The post... their ends drooped or curled up. All of the colors ran together. Paint dripped down, and the places where markers had been used were all streaked and splotchy. You couldn't read any of the words. The pictures of the candidates had colorful smears, making them unrecognizable. It looked like a wall of kindergartners' finger paintings.

"I don't want to be a critic or anything, but these posters are kind of hard to read," Ringo said. "The colors are pretty, though," he added hastily.

"The candidates didn't do this to their posters," I told him. "Someone destroyed them."

"Why would anyone do that?" Ringo asked.

I didn't know the answer to that question. But the tingling sensation in my nose told me I was sniffing around at the edge of a brand-new story.

GET REAL

SERIES

GET REAL #1:
Girl Reporter Blows Lid off Town!

GET REAL #2:
Girl Reporter Sinks School!

GET REAL #3:
Girl Reporter Stuck in Jam!

GET REAL #4:
Girl Reporter Snags Crush!

GET REAL #5:
Ghoul Reporter Digs Up Zombies!

GET REAL #6:
Girl Reporter Rocks Polls!

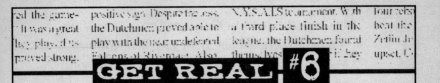

Girl Reporter Rocks Polls!

Created by
LINDA ELLERBEE

AVON BOOKS ◆ NEW YORK

A Division of HarperCollinsPublishers

My deepest thanks to Katherine Drew, Anne-Marie
Cunniffe, Lori Seidner, Holly Camilleri, Whitney
Malone, Roz Noonan, Alix Reid, Julia Richardson,
and Susan Katz, without whom this series of books
would not exist. I also want to thank Christopher
Hart, whose book, *Drawing on the Funny Side of
the Brain*, retaught me how to cartoon. At age 11,
I was better at it than I am now. Honest.

Drawings by Linda Ellerbee

Avon Books® is a registered trademark
of HarperCollins Publishers Inc.

Girl Reporter Rocks Polls!
Copyright © 2001 by Lucky Duck Productions, Inc.
Produced by By George Productions, Inc.

Library of Congress Cataloging-in-Publication Data
Ellerbee, Linda.
    Girl reporter rocks polls! / created by Linda Ellerbee.
        p.   cm. — (Get real ; #6)
    Summary: School newspaper reporter Casey Smith uncovers a plot to
sabotage the elections at her middle school.
    ISBN 0-06-440760-8 (pbk.) — ISBN 0-06-028250-9 (lib. bdg.)
    [1. Newspapers—Fiction.   2. Journalism—Fiction.   3. Elections—
Fiction.   4. Schools—Fiction.]   I. Title.
PZ7.E42845 Ghm   2000   00-32030
[Fic]–dc21   CIP
                                                                         AC

Typography by Carla Weise
1 2 3 4 5 6 7 8 9 10
❖
First Edition

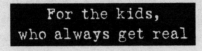
For the kids,
who always get real

Girl Reporter
Rocks Polls!

Adult Hysteria Infects Middle School!

My name is Casey Smith, and I had proof that the grown-ups had cracked. The evidence was right here in my hands.

I stared down at the stack of flyers my homeroom teacher handed me to pass along the row.

To All Parents:

In light of recent tragic events around the country, the PTA has decided to step up school security. As part of a pilot program, we are installing metal detectors at the school entrances. You will be informed of other measures as they are taken.

As always, we welcome your questions and suggestions.

The letter was signed by the principal, Ms. Nachman, and Amy Caldwell, president of the PTA. So this was the reason we'd been sent back to homeroom ten minutes before dismissal? Not that I minded having Spanish cut short. Señora Nuñez had been so thrown that she'd forgotten to assign homework. Too bad.

"What's the holdup?" the boy beside me hissed. He held out his hand for the flyers.

I blinked at him. I had been frozen, midpass. I couldn't help it. This input required processing.

I peeled off the top page and handed him the stack. He took one, gave it a quick scan, and shoved it into his backpack. Then he passed the stack to the next kid.

Metal detectors? Here? That could only mean one thing: They were going to check us—*us!*—for weapons!

Were they nuts? Were they actually planning to treat the kids at Trumbull Middle School like criminals?

Then a second scary thought hit me so hard my eyes bulged. The way they do when I get walloped in the stomach during a game of dodge ball in gym.

Why? I wondered. Did the administration have a noncracked reason to install the metal detectors? Maybe there was a serious problem here. One we knew nothing about.

I wiped my sweaty palms on my red sweat-shirt and took in a couple of deep breaths. Logic returned.

I'm a very observant person. I mean, it's what I *do*. And I'm pretty sure I would have noticed if there were something weird going on at Trumbull—especially something dangerous. It's the kind of thing that would be hard to hide. Rumors spread faster among kids than the flu.

The sudden panic over school safety had to be a case of grown-ups being grown-ups. Hysterical, as usual.

I heard murmuring around me as some of the kids in my homeroom read the flyer. "Ms. Wendall?" someone called from the back. "What's this about?"

Before Ms. Wendall could answer, the bell rang. And no matter how curious we all were about what was going on, most of the kids were far more interested in booking it out of there.

Explanations would have to wait.

Unless I found out the answers myself . . .

There was a definite upside to this metal detector business, I realized. Not only did I feel it in my gut—I felt it in my nose! My nose for news was tingling.

See, I'm a reporter. I may only be a sixth

3

grader in sleepy old Abbington, Massachusetts, but I've still managed to uncover some great stories for our school newspaper, *Real News*. In fact, if it weren't for me and a handful of other gutsy sixth graders, there wouldn't even *be* a newspaper. But that's another story.

As creepy as the idea of needing metal detectors in school might be, it qualified as news. Not the gushy, school spirit, who's-having-a-bake-sale kind of story that Megan O'Connor, the editor in chief, usually goes for. This was hard news. Newsy news.

Real news.

My red hightop Converse sneakers squeaked on the floor as I rushed out of the class. Shoes are my only fashion statement. I have a closet full of Converse sneakers in all different colors. With brown hair, brown freckles and brown eyes, I figure I need a little color in my life.

I headed over to the *Real News* office. At least, I tried to. It was hard to get through the chattering clumps of kids. A crowd clustered near the front entrance.

"Oh, great," said a girl in a wheelchair. "Next thing you know, they'll be searching our lockers."

"They already are!" said a tall girl with spiky blond hair. "Dave told me they're doing random locker searches while we're in class!"

I didn't know them or their friend Dave, but their conversation fueled my story. I squeezed my way through the group. Sometimes being kind of short with pointy elbows comes in handy.

Two men wearing gray uniforms were taking measurements of the front doors and the hall. A man with a clipboard stood talking to a hyper woman in a red suit.

I'd recognize that helmet-head anywhere. That frozen mass of blond hair belonged to Ms. Caldwell, president of the PTA. My grandmother claims that when she sits behind Ms. Caldwell at PTA meetings, she actually gets dizzy from the hairspray fumes.

"You'll have something to check backpacks and purses and things, won't you?" Ms. Caldwell asked.

"Whatever you feel is necessary," the man replied. He jotted down a note on the paper attached to the clipboard.

"Oh, it's necessary," Ms. Caldwell insisted. "In fact, we're thinking of banning backpacks altogether."

My eyebrows shot up. Banning backpacks? How would we live?

"So we'll meet in Principal Nachman's office at four o'clock for a complete assessment," Ms. Caldwell said. Then she wafted down the hall, trailing a cloud of SuperHold hairspray.

A sixth-grade girl leaned against a row of colorful election posters. "Did someone bring a gun to school?" she asked a teacher tearfully.

"No, of course not," the teacher soothed her.

"Then why are they doing this?" another girl demanded.

"So we all stay safe," the teacher assured them. But she didn't look all that certain to me.

"This is totally bogus," an eighth-grade boy standing near me complained to his friends. "Some parent freaked out, and now we all have to suffer."

"What's the big deal?" the tallest boy replied. "Now we have an excuse to be late for class."

I dug my notebook out of my backpack. This was great stuff. I scribbled down everything I had heard.

I snapped my notebook shut with satisfaction. This was going to be some story! And I had been worried that I wouldn't have anything to contribute to today's story meeting.

By the time I got to the *Real News* office, everyone else was already there.

Gary Williams, sportswriter supreme (according to him), tossed wads of neon-green paper into the trash can.

I'd seen those crumpled green clumps somewhere before. Of course! They were campaign flyers. We were in the swing of student council elections, and the candidates were stuffing our lockers with their flyers. Since school elections are just lame popularity contests anyway, I figured Gary was making good use of the wasted paper.

Gary is a good-looking African-American kid who's a maniac about sports. A lot of girls think he's cute. If I squint and pretend I don't know him, I guess I can see why. His dark eyes glitter mischievously, and even I have to admit he has a killer smile. He doesn't do anything for me, though. Know-it-all jocks just aren't my type.

Righteous Ringo, our resident artist and my favorite flake, sat in the corner in some weird yoga position. "Ohm," he said in greeting.

"Ohm fine, how are you?"

"Maintaining," he said. "Trying to, anyway. The world suddenly seems dangerous."

"I know!" I dropped my backpack and notebook onto our polka-dot table, aka Dalmatian Station.

Staff photographer Toni Velez waved a flyer at me, making her multiple bangle bracelets jingle. "So you heard?"

"Heard?" I repeated. "I'm doing a story on it."

"A story on what?" Miss Perfect in Pink, Megan O'Connor, glanced up from her notepad.

7

Her handwriting is so neat I could even read it upside down and backward. I saw my name written in purple ink on the third line down. Right next to the words "Profiles of the Candidates."

Oops. I had forgotten that I'd promised to do those boring profiles for student council president. Well, I wasn't going to back off the school safety story for such a snoozer.

"I bet I know," Gary said. "The metal detectors."

"Wow," I said. "You figured that out without a scorecard. Congratulations. There may be a brain in that jock skull after all."

"Hah hah." Gary tipped back his chair and crossed his arms over his chest. He was wearing a red sports-related jersey advertising some team I've never heard of.

Megan's twinkly blue eyes settled on me. "What about the metal detectors?"

"*Everything* about them!" I exclaimed. "Why the school thinks they're necessary, for one thing. Are we in danger? Or is the administration just torturing us again?"

"And scaring students in the process," Toni added. "Some of the kids are way freaked." She jingled again as she pushed back her wild, orange-streaked hair.

Gary laughed. "You're the one who should be

scared, Toni," he teased. "The metal on you[r] arms today would set off those alarms. Pronto."

Toni scowled at him, then laughed. "My mom says my fashion sense can be pretty *alarming*. But I don't think this is what she meant."

Megan's pale brows came together over her blue eyes. "You're right, Casey," she said. "Installing metal detectors in our school is news."

Wow. I don't think Megan and I have ever agreed on a story so easily.

She pointed her purple pen at me. "But don't forget. You're also covering the elections."

"I was wondering," I wheedled. "Can Gary take care of the election story?"

Megan swiveled in her seat to look at Gary. "Actually, I'd like *you* to do a story on the Brain-Busters team."

Gary brought his chair back down with a thud. "No way," he protested.

"I don't blame you," Ringo said. "They sound scary." He shuddered. "How exactly do they bust brains?"

"*Brain-Busters* is a cable TV game show," I explained.

"You watch that geek parade?" Gary raised an eyebrow.

"My gram watches it," I explained.

"She does?" Toni asked.

I could see why she'd be surprised. It's not the kind of thing you'd expect from my gram.

I've got the coolest grandmother. My parents are away, so Gram has been living with me. She's an award-winning journalist and is writing a book. Toni is probably having trouble picturing my kick-butt gram kicking back in front of a show aimed at kids. It's tough for *me* to imagine—and I've seen her do it. She even yells answers at the screen.

"Gram says she likes the fact that kids are being rewarded for having brains," I told them.

Brain-Busters is like *Jeopardy* for brainiacs. They ask the kinds of questions that you might get on superhard final exams in the accelerated program. School teams compete against each other. Only the teams who make it into the regional finals get to compete on the show. The winners get college scholarship money and funds for the schools.

Its appeal is a total mystery to me. Pop quizzes make me sweat. And kids actually volunteer for this agony.

"But why should *I* cover it?" Gary asked. "It's not a sport."

"It's a *team*," Megan countered.

Gary snorted. "That's not the same thing."

"It kind of is," Ringo said. "Ooh. Brain exercise."

"What?" I asked, watching him unfold from his pretzel position on the floor.

Ringo grabbed his pad and a marker and did a quick sketch. "Here's a question: What would a brain look like perfoming on the parallel bars?"

"Come back from your parallel universe," Gary said.

"Hold on," I said. "I think there's a Simon brewing."

"Fully percolated." Ringo handed the cartoon to Megan.

Megan smiled. "It's great," she said, passing it around. "It will be perfect with Gary's story."

MENTAL GYMNASTICS

Gary laughed at the cartoon. "That's cool. But I still don't think I should be the one to cover the Brain-Busters."

"What's wrong, Gary?" I asked. "You'll only write about games where kids hurt each other and get sweaty?"

Gary ignored the diss. "Nobody knows any of the kids on the team," he complained. "Why would anyone want to read about them?"

Gary had a point. When they posted the list of kids who qualified I hadn't recognized a single name. Of course, I don't run with the Brains.

"The fact that Trumbull has a team is news," Megan said. "They might even end up on TV. That's exciting—and their friends will want to read about it."

"Do those kids actually have any friends?" Gary said with a smirk.

"Of course they do," Megan said. "Everyone has friends."

Maybe they did in Megan-land. Out here in the real world, there were plenty of lonely kids. Ringo wasn't the only one living in a parallel universe. Megan was equally out of touch, it seemed to me.

"Okay, okay," Gary grumbled.

Megan beamed. "Great. Now, I want to wrap up this meeting. I have to be somewhere."

"What do you mean, you have to be some-where?" I demanded. "Which one of your many activities is more important than a *Real News* meeting?"

Megan readjusted her pink velvet headband, smoothing back her blond hair. A totally unneces-sary move, since her hair was perfect, as always. "If you must know, I was invited to tea."

"Tea?" Toni snorted. "What kid has tea parties?"

I rolled my eyes and tipped my head toward Megan. "Duh. Kids like Megan."

I could just see Megan at a tea party, sur-rounded by a pack of ruffled frill-heads. Half the time Megan dressed as if she were Alice in Wonderland waiting for the Mad Hatter and the Dormouse to show up.

"In England they drink tea instead of coffee," Ringo commented.

Ringo has this really cool friend Melody who moved here from London. Now he's up on things Britannia.

"I guess that means instead of coffee breaks they have tea breaks," he continued. "And eat tea cakes instead of coffee cakes. Use teaspoons instead of coffee spoons."

"Ringo, *we* have teaspoons," I pointed out.

"Oh yeah. Do you think that's a holdover from when we were a British colony?" Ringo asked.

"I don't know." Sometimes following Ringo's tangents makes my head hurt. "So who is this tea with, Megan," I prodded. "The Queen of England?"

"Not 'arf likely," Ringo said in his fake accent. "Her Majesty is back at the palace."

"Willa Greenberg and Stacy Carmel invited me," Megan said. She said their names as if she was announcing the members of the Pulitzer committee. Or, to use a reference closer to Megan's heart, the members of *NSYNC.

"You're hanging with the eighth graders?" Toni asked Megan.

Gary studied Megan with an admiring expression. "So you've been tagged by Willa? Way to move up, Megan."

Megan sucked in her lower lip as if she was trying to keep herself from bursting into song.

"What do you mean?" I asked Gary. "What's the big deal?" I couldn't figure out why Toni and Gary were making such a fuss. You'd have to kidnap me to get me to go to a tea party.

"Hello? Willa's crew kind of rules the school, Casey," Gary said. "I'd think a reporter would know who the power players are."

"Oh, please. Willa Greenberg is just *popular*." I said the *p* word with my best sneer. And I have an excellent sneer. I've practiced it a lot. "That doesn't make her important."

"Willa and Stacy and their friends are on a lot of committees," Megan pointed out. "They're really involved in what goes on in this school."

"Right," I said sarcastically. Something else I've practiced a lot. "I can just hear them now." I made my voice supersquealy. "Ooh, what color should the yearbook cover be? Ooh, should we have pink carnations or red carnations for the Valentine's Day assembly?" I leaned back and put my feet up on the table. "Big whoop."

"I vote for pink," Ringo said. "Wait." His face crinkled in a puzzled frown. "Is it already time for Valentine's Day? How did I miss Thanksgiving, Christmas, Chanukah and Kwanzaa?"

Megan's blue eyes narrowed as she looked at me. "Just because someone is popular doesn't mean they're stupid," she said.

"Megan has a point, girl," Toni agreed. "After all, Megan is popular *and* she's sharp."

"Thanks," Megan said. She gave Toni a warm grin. Toni sent back her closest approximation. Toni doesn't do warm fuzzy. She's more cool prickly.

"Megan's going to be even more popular now that Willa Greenberg and Stacy Carmel are inviting her to parties," Gary said.

"The tea is for everyone on the yearbook committee," Megan explained. "It's no biggie."

15

The way she said it made it clear it *was* a biggie. At least to her.

"So can we please finish this meeting?" Megan asked.

"Oh, Gary." Natalie Klein singsonged from the doorway. A big smile spread across her face, every pearly white aimed at our resident jock.

Natalie was on the swim team, and I was pretty sure she had a crush on Gary. The way he smiled made me think maybe he was crushed back.

"Hey, Natalie. Excellent meet last week," Gary said.

"Thanks." Natalie's smile grew even bigger—if that was possible. How much wider could her smile get before her face cracked? "Listen, can you come over here? I want to ask you something."

The tiniest blush tinted Gary's coffee-toned cheeks. He ran a hand over his flat-top. Another totally unnecessary hair-fix gesture.

Gary stood and headed to the doorway. He didn't walk. He did not shuffle. He strutted.

Natalie whipped out a huge pink Super Soaker water gun. "Wet is wild!" she shrieked. She sent a stream of water shooting into the newsroom.

"Gotcha!"

Swimmers Strike with Watery Weapon!

"EEK!" MEGAN DUCKED under the table to avoid the spray.

Toni lunged to protect her camera. "Are you nuts?" she snapped.

"Hey, I already had a shower," I complained. I grabbed my notebook, but I was safely out of the line of fire. I noticed that Megan's notes were now a purple splotch. Luckily, Ringo had moved his sketch to the computer table.

"Wh-wh-" Gary pulled his sopping wet jersey away from his body. He was completely drenched.

Natalie cracked up. I could hear another girl giggling hysterically in the hallway behind her.

"The girls on the swim team made a dare," Natalie gasped. She was laughing so hard she had to hang on to the wall to keep from falling over.

It was funny, but it wasn't *that* funny.

"We all have these Super Soakers, and"—she gulped in some more air—"and we each had to soak a boy. So I soaked you!"

Janelle Watson, the invisible giggler, popped her head into the room. "And I'm her witness," she declared.

"So—gotcha, Gary!" Natalie chirped. She grabbed Janelle's hand, and they raced down the hall, laughing like hyenas on helium.

"And now I'm going to get you!" Gary raced out of the room after them.

Megan climbed back out from under the table. "Oh, no," she cried, noticing the soggy mess that used to be her notebook. She pulled a pack of tissues out of her backpack and tried to mop up the pages.

"They should all have their heads soaked," I muttered. I grabbed some of Megan's tissues and wiped up the table.

"But Natalie and Janelle are on the swim team," Ringo said. "They're soaked every afternoon."

I sighed. "Whatever." I tossed the wet clump of tissues into the trash.

"If we could please finish?" Megan said. "So it's settled. Casey, you'll take care of the election."

"No one cares about this stupid election," I

complained. "It's all just a popularity contest."

"Who's running?" Toni asked.

Megan thought for a minute. "Well, Willa."

"You see?" I said. "The only candidate you can think of is Miss Popularity. How can anyone else have a chance?"

"Then it's even more important to report on the candidates," Megan said. "To level the playing field."

I could tell there was no way for me to get out of this. In order to write the school safety story, I'd have to cave and do the stupid profiles.

Wait a second. This election might not be so boring after all! This was no brainless "What should our mascot be" election year. We had a serious subject here. What was the right balance between safety and personal freedom at school? In addition to the metal detectors, that walking hairdo, Ms. Caldwell, had mentioned banning backpacks. I had even overheard some kids saying that the school might start doing random locker searches.

Issues. They're what make election coverage interesting. And if the candidates didn't realize that now they'd have to take a stand, well, I'd make sure they did!

"Sorry I'm late." Our faculty advisor, Mr.

Baxter, rushed in. It never fails to amaze me how quickly such a round guy can move. He always seems to be in a hurry.

"We were wrapping up our story assignments," Megan said.

"Good. Good." Mr. Baxter dropped his stack of folders onto the table. Just by luck he managed to avoid the puddle left by Natalie's water attack.

"We thought we'd feature the Brain-Busters team," Megan told him.

"I'm covering the installation of the metal detectors, with a look at school safety," I put in. I didn't want him to think we didn't recognize a hot story when we saw one.

"Remember to report, not editorialize," Mr. Baxter warned. It's kind of a mantra with him. Though for some reason, he seems to only use it on me.

"Casey is *also* writing about the school election," Megan added pointedly. "We'll have more ideas tomorrow."

"You may not need them," Mr. Baxter said.

That made me sit up straight. My "uh-oh" radar was on alert. "Why not?" I asked.

"The yearbook committee petitioned for more money," Mr. Baxter explained. "They'd like to use color photos for the graduating class, and they need new printers and a copier."

"That's for sure," Megan piped up. "The yearbook copier leaves a shadowy line running right down the middle of each page. It looks terrible."

"Their computers are even more ancient than ours," Toni agreed.

I stared at her.

She shrugged. "Hey, they need photographers, too," Toni said. "I checked them out."

I couldn't believe Toni would get involved with those popularity drones on the yearbook committee. She would definitely stand out in that cookie-cutter crowd.

"That's great news," Megan said. "The yearbook will be even better this year."

Mr. Baxter leaned against the wall. The man is not a sitter. I've seen him perch, lean, and hover. I guess he never stays in one place long enough to land. Or he's too round to bend. "Well, here's the thing," he said.

I glared at him. "What's the thing?" I demanded.

"The money has to come from somewhere," he explained. "So it's coming out of the *Real News* budget."

"What!" I shrieked. I slammed my hand down on the table. Eew. Right in the puddle.

Gary strolled back into the room. He was even wetter than before, but he had a big grin on his face. Then he caught my expression.

"Whoa," he said. "Who died?"

"*Real News*," I declared.

Newspaper to Die
Sudden Death!

"DON'T EXAGGERATE, CASEY," Mr. Baxter said. He opened his briefcase and pulled a bologna sandwich out of it, then took a bite. How could he eat at a time like this?

"What's Casey talking about?" Gary asked.

Mr. Baxter's eyes traveled from Gary's wet hair to his soaked T-shirt and then back again. "Is it raining down the hall, Mr. Williams?"

"Uh, I, well . . ." Gary stammered. "It's kind of a long story."

"I'm sure it is. Luckily, I don't have time to hear it."

What was wrong with these people? Why were they talking about this stupid stuff? "How can you kill *Real News*?" I demanded.

"If you would allow me to get in a word,

Casey?" Mr. Baxter put down his sandwich and wiped his mouth with a napkin. "We are not 'killing *Real News*,' as you so dramatically put it. We're just putting the new computers on hold—"

"Great," I muttered. "That's a big comfort."

Mr. Baxter gave me a look that said "stop interrupting." So I did. "And we will have to trim the paper a bit."

"No!" I gasped. "How can you do that?"

Mr. Baxter ignored my outburst. "We'll publish fewer pictures—"

At that, I heard Toni snap her chewing gum.

"—and some of the issues will be shorter." He held up a hand to keep me from interrupting again. "Some issues, Casey, not all. You'll see. It's not that big a deal."

"Not a big deal!" I shouted. At a teacher. But I didn't care. I was so mad I could chew spoons and spit steak knives. Luckily, Mr. Baxter is pretty cool about that kind of thing. "This is terrible! Why should they get our money?"

"The yearbook and *Real News* are both journalism," Mr. Baxter replied. "It makes perfect sense that they share the budget."

"Perfect sense?" I barked. "To who?"

"Whom," Megan corrected.

My body tensed. Every muscle prepared to fly across the table. Megan's blond hair was the perfect length to wrap around her neck.

Toni grabbed my wrist. "Down, girl," she ordered. "Nothing gets solved that way."

Since I couldn't strangle the editor in chief and I definitely wasn't allowed to kick our faculty advisor in the shins, I paced.

"The yearbook is *not* journalism." I ranted. "Not even close. No one ever made the evening news with a spread on the lunchroom ladies. Profiles of the Microchips club never changed the world."

"Calm down, Casey," Mr. Baxter said.

I hate it when grown-ups tell me to calm down. Especially in the middle of a crisis. It has the opposite effect on me.

Mr. Baxter swallowed some more of his bologna sandwich. "Keep in mind, things had to be shuffled around to create a budget for *Real News*. It wasn't an existing club until you kids decided to revive it this semester. This year, *Real News* makes the compromise. Next year, the year-book budget will accommodate you."

"Next year?" I couldn't think that far ahead. "What about *this* year? We're just getting *Real News* off the ground."

"Look on the bright side," Mr. Baxter replied. "Now there will be less pressure on you to come up with so many stories for each issue."

My jaw dropped. He didn't understand me at

all. Reporters thrive under that pressure. Meeting that challenge is what I do. It's in my blood. I need it to live. And now I was being told I have to ration my supply. He might as well tell me to breathe less, or give up my white blood cells and hang in there with just the red ones.

Mr. Baxter wadded up his napkin and sandwich bag and threw them into the garbage can. I felt as if he was tossing *Real News* in the can, too.

"Keep me posted on the next issue," he said. He gathered up his folders and waddled out. Double time.

I stared after him. My ears were hot. My blood was cold. My freckles radiated fury. Even my hair was mad.

I spun on my heel and glared at Megan. "This is all your fault."

She looked shocked. "How is it my fault?" she asked. "I had nothing to do with it."

I wagged my finger in her face. "The kids on the yearbook committee are the popular kids. So they get everything they want."

"Even if that was true, it still wouldn't make it my fault," Megan protested. "I'm as bugged about cutting the *Real News* budget as you are."

What a phony. "Oh really?" I challenged her. "Bugged enough to make your yearbook pals give us the money back?"

Megan stared at me as if I was crazy. "I don't have that kind of power. Only the student council makes those decisions. And it already made one."

I flung myself into a chair and glared at the computer screen. I knew she was right. I just wasn't ready to admit it. Not out loud.

There was an awkward silence in the room. I suspected everyone was afraid to say anything that might set me off. Which was fine by me, because I could actually feel steam blasting out of my ears. One wrong word from anyone and I didn't think I could control myself.

So I did what any reporter does when facing disappointment and disaster. Research.

I logged on to the school website and clicked onto the student council minutes. I wanted to see for myself how those creeps had chiseled away at our budget.

I pick at my scabs, too.

My eyes widened as I read the minutes from the student council meeting. My eyes locked on two names on my PC monitor—Willa and Stacy— the budget bandits. "Well, well, well," I murmured. "Looky here."

"What?" Megan asked behind me.

"Guess who lobbied for the reallocation of funds?" I asked back. "Your brand-new best friends, Willa and Stacy."

"Really?" Megan leaned over my shoulder to read the screen.

"Those self-serving rats!" I exclaimed. I whirled around in my chair so fast Megan stumbled backward. "The people benefitting most from this change were the exact same people to push it through. Ever hear the phrase *conflict of interest*?"

Megan bit her lip. "Um. . . ."

"Gee. Don't have an answer for that one, do you?" I stood up and pointed at the screen. "And double gee, both Willa and Stacy are running for office."

I stalked to Dalmatian Station and picked up my stuff. "Triple gee," I continued, slinging the backpack over my shoulder. "I wonder what the student body will think of candidates who use their positions in student government to their own advantage. Because I'm writing up Willa and Stacy—and don't try to stop me!"

Megan just sat down in my chair and squinted at the computer screen. She didn't try to stop me. Weird.

"Well, I think we're done here." I glanced around the room. Ringo, Toni and Gary all just stared at me. "Oh, and Megan, you better hurry. You don't want to miss your tea party with your budget-stealing friends. Have fun, traitor."

I stormed out.

I felt a little bad about the last part, but only a little. It made a great exit line.

I walked home faster than I thought possible. Feelings tumbled around inside me. One minute I was so angry I could have karate-chopped boards without a pause. The next minute I had to fight back tears. Don't know where they came from. I'm not the weepy type.

We deserved new computers just as much as the yearbook deserved new copiers. So why did they rate instead of us?

Once again, because they were run by the popular clique.

I had never cared much before about who was considered cool and who wasn't. That kind of worry always struck me as such a time-waster. For the first time I saw that being popular had some major benefits. And not being in that clique had some definite consequences.

What was going to happen to *Real News*? Were we going to be trimmed down to just a measly few pages? We had been talking about expanding—running more feature-length stories, adding departments as more kids wanted to get involved. There went that plan.

Another downside flashed though my already short-circuiting brain. Cutting the length of each issue meant more wrangling over which stories were printed. As if there wasn't already enough tension over bylines on a weekly basis.

And what would happen to Toni's awesome pictures? We'd either have to print them so small they wouldn't count or print fewer of them. She always had one toe out the door. Maybe she'd bolt for good, which would be terrible. I needed her on the staff—she was spice to Megan's sugar.

"It's not fair!" I shouted, and kicked a rock. *"Ow!"* I bent down and grabbed my foot. My big toe throbbed. Perfect.

CHAPTER

4

Girl Reporter Breaks Tooth Biting Down on Budget!

THE FIRST THING I did when I got home was e-mail my friend Griffin. Even though he moved mucho miles away, he's still totally hardwired into my life. We connect in the virtual world almost every day—sometimes more than that. I seriously vented. The good thing about e-mail is that I could get it all out without bursting Griff's eardrums.

I dragged myself downstairs for dinner and related the whole sad, infuriating story to Gram. She was sympathetic, but she took Mr. Baxter's side, which really irritated me.

"In the real world, honey, there are always budget crunches." She stabbed a steamed dumpling with a chopstick and dunked it into the Szechuan hot sauce.

We were having Chinese takeout for dinner. Gram is pretty hopeless in the kitchen, which is fine by me. After all, those take-out restaurants would go out of business if it weren't for us. We see our dependence on takeout as a way to support small businesses. Our civic duty.

Gram smiled. "Budgets . . . ha! You should have seen some of the arguments we had at the paper."

"Yeah, well, you were probably always on the winning side," I said. "It's a lot different being on the losing end."

"Thanks for the vote of confidence, but no, I've had my share of disappointments." She popped the whole dumpling into her mouth.

"It's not fair!" I kicked the table leg. "The newspaper is so much more important than that stupid yearbook. The yearbook only matters to the yearbook committee."

"Well, that's probably not strictly true," Gram dished out the rice from a white take-out container. "The yearbook may not cover life-and-death issues, but other kids may like it."

"Right." I scowled. "The kids who are popular enough to get their faces plastered all over it. And the student council backs them up every step of the way. The wrong people are in charge."

"I know it sometimes seems that way," Gram

said. She waggled her chopsticks at me and grinned. "That's why you and I are here—to keep 'em on track! Believe me, adults can be as goofy as kids when it comes to priorities."

That reminded me. "You're not kidding. I think the head of the PTA and the principal have cracked." I dumped a spoonful of Kung Pao chicken onto my pile of rice.

"What has the administration done this time?"

Gram knows that sometimes the Trumbull powers-that-be and I don't quite manage to do the eye-to-eye thing.

"They're installing metal detectors at school," I told her.

Gram froze in the middle of reaching for one of my dumplings. "They're *what*?"

She looked shocked. I guess this was news to her, too. And she goes to all the PTA meetings and everything.

"We got this flyer about it," I explained. "There were security guys there measuring and taking notes and stuff."

"The subject came up at the last PTA meeting," Gram said. "But the decision was tabled pending further information."

"Like what kind of information?" I asked.

"How much the clunkers would cost, for one thing," Gram said. "Not to mention whether or not it's the right thing to do."

"The flyer made it sound like it was a done deal," I said. I got up and headed for my room to get my backpack. "Don't steal my last dumpling," I called over my shoulder.

"What last dumpling?" Gram replied, her mouth full.

I rummaged around in my backpack and pulled out the flyer. I brought it over to Gram.

I looked at my plate and then at Gram's guilty face. "You owe me one dumpling," I told her.

"You stole my last five French fries last night," she protested. "I figure now we're square."

I finished the rest of my Kung Pao chicken while Gram read the flyer.

"I'm going to make some phone calls about this," Gram decided. "Amy Caldwell is moving too quickly for my taste."

I felt better knowing that Gram was on the case. I have to confess, the whole metal detector question was freaky. It opened up so many questions. I knew Gram would give me straight talk on the safety subject.

Gram cleared away the empty containers while I scraped the dishes and then popped them into the dishwasher. Then she headed off to make phone calls, and I went to my room to write up the budget story. Then I'd get onto the metal detectors. And the candidates' profiles. Sheesh. I had a lot of work ahead of me.

First, I did a quick check of my e-mail. Two messages!

To: Wordpainter
From: Thebeast
Re: UNFAIR!!!!!!!!!!!!!!!!!!
    Cutting down the paper totally rots. And you can tell them I said so!
    Griff
    PS Any of your stories get squeezed out of the mini version of REAL NEWS—just send on over to me. I'm your biggest fan.
    G

I smiled at the screen. He always knew exactly how to make me feel better. I sent him a quick reply:

To: Thebeast
From: Wordpainter
Re: Why you're my best bud
    You can always make me go from :(to :)

I was about to click on to my next message when the phone rang.

"Casey, it's for you!" Gram called.

Could it be Tyler? For one second the thought crossed my mind. And I am embarrassed to admit that my heart suddenly did this weird thump-thumpty-thump syncopation.

Tyler McKenzie is in my grade and lately in my radar. Something about his crooked grin makes me all woogly. For a while he hated me, but he seems to have gotten past that. The *Real News* staff is always teasing me about him, which is totally immature and off base.

I picked up the extension in the living room. "I got it!" I hollered. I took a deep breath. "Hello?"

"Hi, Casey."

A wave of disappointment swept through me. It was immediately followed by an equally powerful wave of irritation. "What do you want, Megan?"

"I just wanted to make sure you were all right. You were so upset this afternoon—"

I cut her off. "Do you blame me?"

"No, of course not!" Her voice gushed sincerity. Okay. She probably did really mean it. It's just that hearing her voice made all the frustration of this afternoon come right back, like a bad burrito.

"Casey, I did talk to some of the yearbook staff about what happened."

That shocked me speechless. Megan managed to surprise me again. "Wh-what did you say?"

"Well, I just asked about the budget, and how I wished there was some other way to get the money for the new printers and copiers and everything."

"Really?"

"Casey, don't you get it? *Real News* matters to me, too."

"So what did they say?"

"Well, Willa agreed it was a shame, so you see, she's not as terrible as you think."

"Megan . . ." I did not want to hear her defend that example of all that can go wrong with pretty, popular girls.

"I just wanted to make sure you weren't still mad at me."

I let her dangle for a minute. Finally I said, "Well, I take back what I said at the meeting. I don't really think this is your fault."

"Thank you." I could hear her relief. It surprised me that Megan cared so much about what I thought. "And I want you to know I understand why you got so mad," she added.

"Okay." There was a long pause. I wondered if I was supposed to say something else. I couldn't think of anything. "Okay?" I repeated.

"Okay." Megan replied. "See you tomorrow. And get to work on those candidate profiles."

She had to get her editor zing in. "Yeah, yeah, yeah."

We hung up. I felt better. It was probably just hearing from Griffin, but the big bad blechs had started lifting.

I clicked on to my next message.

To: Wordpainter
From: DrMom
Re: How ARE you?

Clean your room, eat more vegetables, stand up straight. There, got all the mom-isms out of the way.

So, sweetie, how are you? I get regular reports from Gram, but could do with a few more words from my favorite daughter.

I have an errand for you. We need a new video camera. The heat and humidity over here didn't agree with our old one. Can you drag Gram to the mall to get us a new one? And how about a special video postcard from you? I'd love a day-in-the-life-of-Casey documentary! We're all really missing you—even Billy (though don't let on that I told you!). Daddy sends his love, too.

Write soon! [Don't make me ask you twice, young lady! ;-)]

XXXXXXX,
Mom

I guess I should explain about my unusual family circumstances. Gram lives with me because my parents, who are doctors, are part of a program called Doctors Without Borders. They travel all over the world, wherever doctors are needed. "Crisis Control" could be on their business cards. Right now they were in Southeast Asia. My sixteen-year-old brother, Billy, went with them. Another example of crisis control— his grades were in the basement, and they wanted to keep an extraclose eye on him during his rebellious years.

I knew why Mom had asked me instead of Gram about the video camera. Gram is allergic to the mall. She would probably tell Mom to just order a camera online. Mom's the kind of shopper who has to see, touch, examine, take apart and compare in person.

I guess Mom figured there is strength in numbers. If Gram and I went together, it would make it a better experience all 'round. So a trip to the mall would have to be scheduled as An After-School Activity Suitable for Child and Designated Caretaker.

I thought about writing to Mom about the metal detector question, but then decided it would only worry her.

Instead, I wrote up my scathing article about

how Willa and Stacy had used their positions as class reps to their own personal advantage. My fingers flew over the keys. Now I know what Gram means when she says that sometimes a story just writes itself!

Then I logged on to the Internet to do all the research I could on school safety. The whole time I worked, the tip of my nose tingled. A wonderful feeling.

I was onto a story!

Popularity Machine Mangles Candidates!

I WOKE UP feeling 2,000 percent better. The Willa-Stacy funding story rocked—and would definitely rock their popularity world. And thanks to the school safety issue, the profiles of the candidates would actually have some substance.

I had woken up extra early to keep doing research. I logged on and scrolled through sites devoted to school safety. I was uncovering some scary stuff. Serious problems, sometimes turning into serious violence.

The whole issue of school safety was really a reaction to violence in schools. And though I'd read about the terrible shootings at Columbine High School in Littleton, Colorado, that was just one incident. My notebook was loaded with examples:

February 1997, Moses Lake, Washington. Junior-high student walks into algebra class with rifle. Kills teacher and two students.

May 1998, Springfield, Oregon. Boy opens fire in school cafeteria, killing 2 and injuring 22.

March 1998, Jonesboro, Arkansas. Two boys, ages 13 and 11, shoot and kill 4 students during a fire drill.

This could never happen at Trumbull, I thought as I stared at the screen. Then my stomach twisted.

No one at Columbine or Jonesboro thought they were in danger either. And a six-year-old bringing a gun to school and shooting another six-year-old? In *America*?

I shivered. Suddenly the issue seemed very real. And what I was finding out was that no one seemed to agree on what to do about the problem.

This was giving me the serious heebies. I logged off and reread my story about the yearbook funding. Reading one of my finished stories always made me feel like the world was a manageable place. Yup! Not a *t* left uncrossed; not an *i* left undotted. Excellent!

I smelled burned toast, so I figured breakfast was ready. Our toaster is temperamental and needs to be watched. Gram never bothers. Maybe we should pick up a new toaster along with the video camera.

"Hey, Gram." I slid into a chair and took a swig of OJ.

"Back at you." She plopped a bowl of instant oatmeal in front of me. I didn't see any toast, so I guessed it was past saving. "You're looking much more chipper this morning."

I tried to talk around the gloppy spoonful of oatmeal in my mouth. "I roh a fory."

Gram raised an eyebrow at me.

I swallowed. "I wrote a story. One that will blow those popularity princesses out of the water."

Gram sat down across from me and took a sip of coffee. "Hm."

I couldn't tell if that was a disapproving "Hm" or a not-a-morning-person "Hm." "What?" I demanded.

"Just be sure you're not carrying out some kind of personal vendetta," Gram warned. "Even

43

popular kids deserve fair coverage."

"I know that!" I protested.

"Facts are most powerful when they're presented in a calm, evenhanded way," she lectured.

"I know how to write a story," I reminded her. "Reporter objectivity. Blah blah blah."

She smiled. "And I know how passionate my granddaughter can get. Which is just fine by me."

"Did you find out more about the metal detectors?" I asked.

"Amy Caldwell has gone into high gear," she said. "She'll present her findings at the PTA meeting next week."

"Do you think they'll go for it?" I asked. It was hard to imagine what it would be like to have to walk through those things every morning.

"Frankly, I think it's going to depend on what happens in the news over the next few weeks. Most of the parents I spoke to do feel it's an extreme measure to take."

"I'm going to write a story about it," I told her as the phone rang.

"I think that's great. You should come with me to the PTA meeting next week."

My mouth was full so I just nodded.

Gram kissed the top of my head as she went to answer the phone. I could tell she was talking to her publisher.

Gram is writing the story of her life—that's how cool she is. I hope someday some muckety-muck in New York will be dying to read my memoirs. Of course, something interesting will have to happen to me first.

This was turning into a long phone call. I downed my OJ, dropped the oatmeal bowl and spoon in the sink and packed up my stuff for school.

Gram was still on the phone when I was ready to leave. I left her a note:

Dateline: Tuesday before school

Who: You and Me

What: A search mission

Where: The mall (cringe)

When: After school

Why: Mom and Dad need a new video camera.

There! That should show Gram that I never forget the basics of reporting.

I used a typewriter-shaped magnet to stick the note to the refrigerator. I put on my coat, slung my backpack over my shoulder, waved at

Gram and headed out the door.

The weirdest feeling came over me as I approached the front entrance of Trumbull. I felt nervous. No, more than nervous—I felt scared.

I had never felt afraid of going to school before. Annoyed, bothered and apprehensive maybe—but scared for my life? Never. For a split second, school seemed kind of terrifying.

It's just the research I've been doing, I told myself. It had me spooked. I tried to shake off the willies. These were still the same old doors I'd walked through loads of times in the past few months.

All of a sudden the whole safety issue seemed even more confusing than before. I wanted to feel safe. But were metal detectors and random locker-searches the way to go? I hated to think that Trumbull could become a middle-school prison.

Kids streamed by me. If I stood out here much longer I'd be late. I took a deep breath and strolled in as if nothing was wrong. Because nothing *is*, I reminded myself.

The bell was going to ring any minute. I whipped through the nearly empty hallway, and I slammed right into someone.

"Agh!" A girl toppled to the ground. Papers went flying.

"I'm sorry," I gasped. "I didn't see you." Where did she come from? I hadn't spotted her coming. In fact, I didn't think I'd ever seen her before.

Not that she would stand out in a crowd or anything. She had light-brown hair that was sort of straggly. Khaki pants. A white button-down shirt with a brown sweater over it. Light-brown eyes. Basically, the overall impression was that she was beige. She blended into the wall.

"Are you okay?" I asked.

"It . . . it was my fault," she mumbled. "I wasn't looking where I was going, I guess." She began gathering up her papers.

I bent down to help. "I'm really sorry," I apologized again. I grabbed some papers while the girl reached for her scattered pens.

I glanced at the page on top. It was some kind of flyer. "'Vote for Jodi Dillard for Student Council President,'" I read out loud. Hm. I had never heard of Jodi Dillard. "Oh, here." I held the papers out to the girl.

"Thanks," she said, taking them.

"Gotta go!" I dashed down the hall.

I raced to homeroom. I slipped inside just as the final bell rang. Phew! Just made it.

I got through my morning classes without too many goof-ups. An accomplishment, since I was itching to get started on the school-safety story. I was also a little nervous about how Megan was going to react when I handed in my school-funds story. Her new best friends did not come off very well. Finally the bell rang for lunch, and I headed straight to the *Real News* office.

I tossed my backpack onto Dalmatian Station. I flexed my fingers. I was ready to rock!

"Hi, Casey," Megan greeted me from her computer.

"Uh, hi, Megan." I sat at a computer and loaded in my floppy. I opened up the Willa-Stacy story so I could enter it into the Current Issue folder.

Gary walked in. He glanced back and forth between Megan and me. "Uh-oh. Is it safe to come in here?"

"Don't worry," I promised him. "I'm not going to tear your head off."

"Or soak it," Megan added with a giggle.

If Toni had made that comment I would have high-fived her. Since it was Megan I just stared.

Was Miss Priss actually developing a sense of humor? Teasing Gary about Natalie and the soggy Super Soaking might be evidence that Megan was learning to lighten up. I'd like to think it was my influence.

I'd like to think that—but it probably wasn't true.

Ringo bounced into the room. Literally.

"What are you doing?" Gary asked.

"I want to come up with a cheer from the basketball's perspective," Ringo explained. "The ball is working hard, too. I should know. I bounced here all the way from upstairs."

Toni Velez leaned in the doorway. "What's up?" she asked. "Besides Ringo." She eyed him as he bounced in front of her. Up and down. Up and down.

Toni stepped carefully around Ringo and sat down. "So . . . how's it going?" she asked me uncertainly.

I must have scared them all yesterday. "It's going fine. Now could you all leave me alone so I can work on this story? And Ringo, you're making me dizzy!"

Ringo stopped. "I'm making me dizzy, too. Whoo." He flopped onto a chair.

Megan dragged her chair over to mine. She peered at my screen.

Her eyes narrowed. "This isn't about the election," she said. "Or school safety. You're writing something mean about Willa and Stacy."

"I'm writing the truth about them," I countered. "And it relates to the election. It's not my fault that no one will vote for Willa for student council president or Stacy for rep once they know what they're really like."

"Sounds hot," Toni said. "I'd like to see Willa knocked down a peg."

Megan looked crushed by Toni's comment. But did she yell at her? No. She yelled at me!

"*Real News* isn't a vehicle for your rants, Casey," Megan lectured.

I hate it when she does that. Who does she think she is—a teacher?

"It's a conflict of interest for a student rep to lobby for her specific club," I pointed out. "That's a newsworthy story."

"If the story is well written, and fair, then we'll run it," Megan said reluctantly. "But don't neglect the election coverage. I need those profiles, remember?"

Toni jangled her multiple bracelets. "I'm surprised anyone thinks they have a chance against the popularity machine known as Willa and her pals."

Megan seemed to want to change the subject. She turned around and looked at me. "What about your metal-detector story?"

I bit my lip. "I'm working on it. But I think it will be a better story if I hold off until after the PTA meeting next week. It's bound to be a hot one, and it'll round out my story."

Megan nodded, then scribbled something in

her notepad. "Okay. Gary, how's it going with the Brain-Busters?"

"I'll get on it," Gary promised. "I'll hit their practice after school."

After school. That reminded me. I had to take a side trip to the mall.

And I'd felt scared this morning. Walking into Trumbull Middle School was nothing compared to crawling the mall!

CHAPTER 6

Girl Reporter Opens Mouth, Inserts Video Camera!

GRAM AND I made a surgical strike at the mall. We honed in on the video camera, bought it, and beat it out of there before the Muzak infected our brains permanently.

When I got home I sent Mom a "mission accomplished" e-mail.

> I'm bringing the camera to school tomorrow.
> Documentary evidence of the torture inflicted on me every day . . .

I don't really hate school, but the attitude is kind of expected. I don't want Mom to worry that something is wrong with me.

* * *

The next morning I packed up the video camera. I did a quick scan of the instructions, and it looked really easy. That's how I like my technology: Casey-friendly.

When I kissed Gram good-bye I detected the faint odor of burned toast. Oops. Forgot to suggest buying a new toaster at the mall yesterday. Oh, well.

"Have a good day reporting from the field," Gram said as I headed out the door.

When I got to school, I took the camera out of its case and aimed it at the school entrance. "Welcome to Trumbull Middle School," I said. "Life, as I currently know it." I hoped the built-in mike was picking up my voice.

"Look at me—I'm a movie star!" An obnoxious eighth-grade boy jumped in front of the camera and started waving his arms. He grabbed a passing kid and yanked him into the camera frame. "Ready! Action!" He started giving the kid noogies.

I lowered the camera. "Oh goody," I said sarcastically. "Now I have your moronic behavior recorded for posterity."

The boys laughed and stumbled into school.

"Jerks," I muttered.

I re-aimed the camera. A group of girls strolled into the frame. Anna Zafrani, drama club diva, stood in the center. "Now!" she ordered. The girls all struck poses.

"Can you get out of the way?" I asked. "I'm trying to shoot the school building."

"Why make a film about inanimate objects?" Anna asked. The Diva and her Diva-ettes switched poses. "We're exploring body language and emotions. Okay, girls: anger!"

The Diva and the Diva-ettes struck new poses.

Whoa. I took a step back. They looked like they were ready to murder me.

"Don't call us, we'll call you," I said. I lowered the camera. "I give up," I muttered. I'd have to make my Casey movie when there were fewer students around.

I repacked the camera. I never realized how star-struck middle-school students could be. Geez.

As soon as the bell rang for lunch, I knew exactly what I wanted to film. The *Real News* office.

I pulled the camera out of the case. Oops. The little red Record light was lit. I must have forgotten to turn it off. Great. Thrilling footage of the inside of a camera case. Somehow, I thought, filmmaking is not in my future.

I rewound the tape to the beginning. I didn't mind taping over this morning's footage.

I stepped into the room. "Here we are at command central." I aimed at the table. "Don't let the polka dots scare you. We actually get serious work done here."

Toni sat at Dalmatian Station, peering through a loupe at a contact sheet. She glanced up at the camera. "Girl, get that thing off me!" She turned her back to the camera.

"Miss Congeniality here is our staff photographer, Toni Velez. She thinks a picture is worth way more than a thousand words."

"I'm more of a behind-the-camera type," she protested. "Not in front of it."

I slowly scanned the room, narrating as I went. "That's the computer I wrote my first *Real News* story on. It's kind of Jurassic, but hopefully we'll get new ones soon."

I pointed out the bulletin board. The filing cabinet. The view. But something was wrong.

I wanted to film the heart of *Real News*. The blood, the guts and the brains of the newspaper. In other words, the people.

I turned off the camera. "Where is everybody?" I asked.

Toni shrugged. "Megan popped in to see if anyone had handed in any stories, then beat on out of here. I haven't seen Gary or Ringo."

Stories. I still had to finish the profiles of the candidates. Make that *start* the profiles of the candidates!

I had to get to work. What better place to find candidates than the lunchroom? I might even find something resembling lunch, too.

"Later," I called over my shoulder to Toni.

"Catch you in reruns," she replied, hunching over the contact sheet.

I passed the student activities room. A sheet of paper listed every single candidate, from student council president all the way down to measly sixth-grade reps.

No surprises here, I thought, scanning the list.

Stacy Carmel was running for reelection for eighth-grade class rep. Another one of the popularity patrol, Derek Johnson, was running for the second spot. They were running unopposed. Well, eighth graders could be mindless, but they weren't stupid. Why bother running against those two?

Sprinkled throughout the list were the usual suspects. Katherine Cutter, a Willa Wannabee, was running for seventh-grade rep. I recognized a few of the names of kids running for sixth-grade rep.

My eyes widened. There was one name that surprised me. Natalie Klein, Super Soaker champ, was running for student council president. Why hadn't Gary told me? Besides Willa, the other candidates for president were Dave Tyson and

Jodi Dillard—two unknowns, at least to me.

My nose wrinkled as I entered the school cafeteria. Eew. It was Wacky Wednesday, also known as Mystery Stew Day. I fiddled in my pocket. Good. Enough quarters for a vending machine lunch. Granola bars and Cheetos were in my future.

I pulled out the camera and started filming. "Now here's a scene not for the squeamish," I announced. "Feeding time at Trumbull."

"Taking pictures of the inmates?" a boy at a front table called in my direction. Instinctively I swung the camera his way. I caught a glimpse of an unamused lunch monitor in the frame before I focused on the sixth-grade freakazoid.

I had seen him around. I couldn't have missed him. He was dressed all in black and had spiky hair. Also black, only it was that weird dyed black that's almost purple.

He sat by himself, reading a thick book. I could tell by the garish cover it was not on our reading list. An oversized backpack sat at his feet. I wondered how much it weighed—and how much stuff did a kid need to carry around?

"I'm prisoner 1234," the boy declared for the camera. "Someday these losers are going to regret keeping me here against my will."

How original. Not.

I figured he wasn't the kind of classmate my parents really wanted to see in my home movie. They'd start worrying about who I was hanging out with. Gram and I did not need that kind of grief.

"Unidentified student expresses opinion," I said as I moved away from the loner. Using the camera, I searched the room. I caught sight of Megan. She'd be very reassuring for my parents after the spiky-haired kid.

I had started to head toward her when I realized she was sitting with Willa Greenberg. I also recognized the other kids at the table. Stacy Carmel, as usual. She and Willa were like Siamese twins. Annoyance times two.

Katherine Cutter was there, too. A moon orbiting the Willa-Stacy sun.

What did Megan see in those girls? Did she want to be popular so much that she'd put up with that trio of airheads?

The answer was right in front of the camera. Sitting between Stacy and Willa was Spencer Woodham, the current student council president. Any time Megan got within three feet of Spence she turned as pink as her favorite velvet dress. She had a really bad case of crush.

Of course! A bell rang in my head. The eighth-grade student council kids all pal around together,

I thought. If Megan is with Willa and Stacy, then she gets to hang around with Spencer, too.

Ding ding ding. Right answer.

I'll get Megan on camera when she's not with those twerps, I decided. I swung the camera around again, searching for Ringo.

I knew Ringo's pal Melody had lunch next period, so he was probably chowing with his fellow rah-rahs. Just as I guessed. Ringo sat among the Frosted Cheerios at the cheerleader table. Right behind him was the jock table, Gary's domain.

One of the cheerleaders, Samantha, pointed at me. All the girls huddled together, then whispered something to Ringo.

With a "Whoo-hoo!" they rose in unison. "Go Trumbull!" they chanted, miming pom-pom waving. A few did scissor kicks.

Ringo lifted Samantha into the air. "Trumbull! Trumbull!" she shouted. She flashed a smile directly at the camera. "Go! Go! Go!"

"I'd like to tell her where to go," I mumbled. Oops. I hoped the mike hadn't picked that up.

Ringo lowered Samantha back to the ground and dashed over.

"Hi, Casey," he said. He wore a bright tie-dyed T-shirt under a checked flannel shirt, and I'd never seen so many pockets on a pair of pants before.

"Looking vivid," I said. "Say hi to my mom and dad."

"Hi, Casey's mom and dad," he said. He held up his fingers in a peace sign. "Greetings from Abbington."

Someone held their fingers up behind Ringo's head. Other kids giggled. Two sixth-grade girls pushed their way in front of the camera and shoved their faces at the lens.

"Quit it," I scolded. "You'll fog the lens." Sheesh. What is it about a camera that brings out the idiot in a person?

"Now your turn." Ringo took the camera from me. He opened up the accessories bag slung on my shoulder and pulled out a mike. He plugged in the cord, then handed me the mike. "Speak," he ordered.

I suddenly felt self-conscious. "Uh, so it's me, Casey." Well, duh. It's not as if your parents won't recognize you. "I-I can't think of anything to say," I confessed.

"I guess you're more of an interviewer, not an interviewee," Ringo said.

That's it! "You just gave me a great idea!" I said. "Come on." I charged toward the popular table.

"Where are we going?" Ringo asked. He followed a few steps behind me.

"To interview the candidates." I saw how eager kids seemed to be about being on camera. Kids who weren't me, anyway. It would make these interviews a snap.

A boy in a yellow sweatshirt and jeans stopped me. "Did you say you were interviewing the candidates?" he asked.

The boy was really tall and really skinny. In that yellow sweatshirt he kinda reminded me of Big Bird.

"Yes." I nodded toward Willa. "I was going to start with the front-runner."

The boy gave me a grin that showed his braces. "I hope you're wrong about that. I'm Dave Tyson. I'm running against her."

Open mouth, insert video camera.

Invisible Kids Spotted in School Cafeteria!

"SORRY," I SAID hastily. "Uh, Ringo, why don't you get a good shot of Dave? I'll just ask a few questions."

"Sure thing," Dave said. He ran a hand through his light-brown hair. He cleared his throat. I held out the mike to him. "I'm Dave Tyson, and I want to be the next president of the student council."

"Why?" I asked.

His face got serious. "In some ways I'm just another average middle-school kid. That means I can represent the average kid's interests better than my opponents. Student government shouldn't just be for the most popular and the most visible kids."

My eyes bugged. Had this guy been reading my mail?

"Yeah," Ringo said from behind the camera. "Someone has to be there for the invisible kids. Their votes are really hard to count, since you can't see them."

"Are you on any school committees or teams here?" He didn't strike me as a jock—more brains than brawn. Actually, I thought, eyeing his lanky frame, this guy was all brains and zippo brawn.

A broad grin spread across Dave's face. "I was just voted captain of the Brain-Busters team," he declared proudly.

Well, that proved he was smart. But it could hurt his chances if it marked him as King of the Nerds.

Then I thought this was the perfect opportunity to start in on the serious issues. "What do you think about installing metal detectors in school?"

Dave's eyes glittered. "Totally against it! They cost a fortune, and this school is having enough budget problems as it is."

"Safety is important," I said. "How would—"

He cut me off. "Not at the expense of personal freedom! The administration wants to force us to line up like cattle to start our school day. I'll do everything I can to stop it!"

"Well, thanks," I said. "I need to go talk to the other candidates before lunch is over."

"Can I send you a memo on my views?" he asked. "Maybe you'd like to publish it in *Real News*."

Memo? My eyebrows raised. Is this guy for real? I wondered if he had a campaign manager and a campaign fund.

"Whatever." I turned to Ringo. "Come on, camera dude."

"Right-o-rama," Ringo said.

I strolled over to Willa's table. Katherine Cutter had vanished. Maybe she had finally come to her senses and abandoned those clones.

Too bad the same couldn't be said for Megan.

Megan shrank down in her chair as if she was trying to disappear. She wouldn't even look at me. That made me mad. It was like she wanted to pretend she didn't know me, just because she was sitting with her popular pals.

"Well, Willa," I said. "Looks like you have some serious competition in the upcoming election."

Willa's eyes narrowed. "You mean that dorky new guy, Dave?"

"This is Willa's third year at Trumbull," Stacy pointed out. "And she's been on student council as rep for two. I think she knows a little bit more about this school than he does."

"Willa would make a great president," Spencer added. "I know what it takes, and she's got it."

This little love fest made me want to barf.

"Cool shot," Ringo murmured. "Willa, you look really good upside down."

"Why are you filming this?" Willa asked.

"Casey is doing profiles of each of the candidates for *Real News*," Megan explained.

Wowie. She just admitted she knew my name.

"Oh, right." Ringo adjusted the camera. "I need to get Willa's profile. Turn sideways, please."

Willa took the mike from me and smiled sweetly at the camera. "If I am elected I will do everything in my power as student council president to make this school a better place."

I grabbed the mike back. "How, exactly?" I asked.

Willa looked flustered. "What?"

"What do you have in mind? Will it be your policy that all students must be color coordinated?"

"Casey," Megan said in a warning tone.

"Willa cares about what goes on in school," Spencer assured me.

"What do you think of the installation of metal detectors?" I asked her.

Willa's smile never wavered. "Anything the administration decides is fine with me. After all, they know what's best for us."

Gag. What a suck-up. "Does that include random locker searches? Banning backpacks?"

"I never use a backpack," Willa said. "It wrinkles my clothes."

"That's not the point." Typical. I ask about something as serious as school safety and she responds with a fashion don't.

Katherine returned to the table. "Here's your chocolate milk," she said. She put the carton on Willa's tray.

Willa didn't even say thank you. She just handed her tray to Katherine. "I'm done with this."

Katherine paused for one second. Please throw it at Willa's head, I prayed.

No such luck. Katherine took the tray. She plastered a big smile on her face. "Anyone else?" she chirped.

Spence and Stacy handed Katherine their trays. Megan looked uncomfortable. "That's okay," she said. "I'll bring mine up later."

"Sure thing." Katherine walked away, carrying the trays to the stack by the trash.

Way to be a doormat, Katherine, I thought. What was it about popular kids that let them get away with that kind of thing? I wondered again how Megan could stand to have anything to do with these creeps. Oh, right—Spence.

"Casey, my stomach is speaking to me," Ringo said. "It's telling me I need to eat lunch."

"Okay, I'll take it from here." Watching Willa order Katherine around had made me lose my appetite anyway. Ringo handed me back the camera and rejoined the rah-rahs.

Two more presidential candidates to go: Natalie and the mystery girl, Jodi Dillard. As I wandered through the lunchroom I asked kids about the election. Their responses depressed me. Then they made me angry.

"Why are you writing a news article?" an eighth-grade girl asked. "Everyone knows Willa is going to win."

"Why should we vote?" her friend added. "The student government doesn't have any real power anyway."

"There's a student government?" a sixth grader asked.

Could these kids be any more apathetic?

Then I started asking about school safety. Kids had lots of different opinions. Some said they would feel safer knowing the metal detectors were there. Others complained that kids were being treated like criminals. The idea of banning backpacks made most of them ballistic. No one wanted school to turn into jail.

I tried to keep the camera going while I fiddled

in my backpack for a pencil and a notebook. I wanted to write down some ideas. I almost let the camera get away from me.

"Whoa!" A pair of hands grabbed the camera just before it hit the floor.

Tyler.

"Thanks," I said. I gazed into his velvety brown eyes. I tried to think of something to say, but nothing came out of my mouth. In this case, that was probably a good thing.

"Are you making a documentary?" he asked.

I laughed. Actually, as much as I hated to admit it, I giggled. "I'm interviewing kids about the election."

"It looks like you could use a cameraman," Tyler offered.

Bonus! Things were definitely looking up.

"Do you know who Jodi Dillard is?" I asked. "She's one of the candidates."

Tyler shook his head. "Never heard of her."

"No one has," I said. "It's weird that she would run for school president. Who's going to vote for someone they don't even know by sight?"

"This camera is really cool," Tyler said, aiming it at me. "You look great. Like a front-line reporter."

I think even my toes blushed at that compliment. Then I held my hand up to the lens as Tyler zoomed in for a super close-up.

"Cut it out," I ordered. "I don't need footage of my pores."

I glanced around the lunchroom. Jodi Dillard, where are you? I thought. *Who* are you?

I spotted the beige girl I'd mowed down in the hall. She had a been carrying a Jodi Dillard flyer. A source!

"I see someone who might know Jodi Dillard," I told Tyler.

"Lead on!" Tyler said.

We hurried over to the girl, who was sitting by herself doing homework.

"Excuse me," I said.

She looked up, startled.

"Do you remember me? We met by your locker." I didn't want to have to remind her that I slammed into her. Tyler already suspects I'm a total klutz.

She looked puzzled, then smiled. "Oh right. You knocked me over."

I heard Tyler crack up behind me. Great. "Another victim of Hurricane Casey," he joked. "Welcome to the club."

"Yes, well, you had flyers for Jodi Dillard, right?" I said. "Can you point her out to me? I'm doing interviews with all the candidates, and no one knows who she is."

"Oh." The girl's face flushed. "Um . . . I'm Jodi."

Once again, big Converse in my mouth. She probably didn't want to hear that she was invisible to the entire fourth-period lunch crowd.

"So, Jodi," I said quickly. "I'm interviewing the candidates. Tell me something about yourself."

"I know nobody knows who I am," she blurted out. "But I think I'd be a really good student council president. I really care about the school, and I think elections are really important."

"Me, too," I said.

"I didn't realize that Dave Tyson was going to run," she admitted. "We're in the accelerated math class together. He's really smart."

"Weren't you worried about Willa Greenberg?" I asked, surprised. "That's who most people think will win."

"I know Willa has a lot of friends and they'll all vote for her," Jodi replied. "I thought I might be able to get the rest of the kids."

"Natalie Klein is running, too," Tyler added.

Jodi nodded. "I know. It all seemed like a much better idea a few days ago."

"Are you in any clubs or on any committees?" I asked. I wanted to be sure I asked all the kids the same questions.

Jodi shook her head. "I'm not much of a joiner, I guess."

"What's your stand on installing metal detectors?" I asked.

Jodi thought for a minute. "I don't really feel like I have enough information to answer that. I'd want to have all the facts before leaping to action. We have to be careful not to act out of panic. Obviously school safety is one of the most important issues, but I think any discussion about it should include the people it affects most—the students."

I like the way this girl thinks, I thought. She sounded a lot like Gram. And me!

"Is that it?" she asked. "I need to make some more posters. Since no one seems to know who I am." She sighed.

I flushed a little at that. "Sure."

Jodi stood and gathered her books. "So, 'bye," she said. She hurried away.

"I wonder why she's running," Tyler commented. "She doesn't seem the type." He handed me back the camera. "I'd better book. My class is on the third floor, and Mr. Carruthers hates it if you're even a minute late."

"Thanks for your help," I called after him.

Ringo charged over to me. "Ready to rock?" Ringo and I had English next period, and we usually walked over together.

"Sure thing." I turned the camera back on as

we headed for the exit. "Ringo and Casey, escaping from the lunchroom."

My stomach growled. I realized I'd never eaten lunch. My stomach hadn't forgotten, though.

I stopped at the vending machines near the doors. The spiky-haired boy was still there. He stood slowly and slung his big backpack over his shoulder.

I noticed the lunchroom monitor watching us. If we didn't hurry, we were going to be late.

"Why were you asking all those questions?" the spiky-haired kid asked.

"I'm doing a story about the school elections," I explained.

The kid snorted. "Elections. Like they matter."

I hit the Off switch on the camera and zipped it into its case. Then I fished around in my pockets for some quarters.

"That's a cool camera," the boy said.

"Thanks." I sighed. "I don't know if I got any good shots, though."

"All you have to do is aim and shoot," Ringo assured me.

I shrugged. "It makes me nervous. Maybe I'm not cut out for this kind of thing."

The spiky-haired guy smirked. "Any idiot can shoot with that thing. They're designed that way. Foolproof."

"Well, this idiot doesn't like it," I retorted.

"Point and shoot," the boy instructed. "Point and shoot. That's all there is to it." He turned and walked through the lunchroom doors, repeating "point and shoot," the whole way out.

"Thanks so much for the lesson," I called after him. His superior attitude bugged me. Not to mention his hairdo.

I bought myself a granola bar, and Ringo and I raced out of the lunchroom. Brightly painted campaign posters went by in a blur. Then I realized they really *were* blurry.

"Check this out." We stopped in front of the bulletin board by the main entrance.

"Psychedelic," Ringo murmured.

The posters were a mess. Their ends drooped or curled up. All of the colors ran together. Paint dripped down, and the places where markers had been used were all streaked and splotchy. You couldn't read any of the words. The pictures of the candidates had colorful smears, making them unrecognizable. It looked like a wall of kindergartners' finger paintings.

"I don't want to be a critic or anything, but these posters are kind of hard to read," Ringo said. "The colors are pretty, though," he added hastily.

"The candidates didn't do this to their

posters," I told him. "Someone destroyed them."

"Why would anyone do that?" Ringo asked.

I didn't know the answer to that question. But the tingling sensation in my nose told me I was sniffing around at the edge of a brand-new story.

Is It Art, or
Just a Bunch of Drips?

THE POSTERS LOOKED as if they had been left out in the rain. But no one would have had time to take them down and put them back up during lunch. Whoever damaged them had done it fast.

Could the sprinkler system have gone off?

Not a chance. The floor was dry, except for a few drips under the posters.

Why would anyone ruin the posters? What was the motive here? Figuring out that angle would give me the lead I needed.

For the rest of the day the splotchy posters were the hot topic. It replaced the threat of metal detectors as the focus of conversation. Everyone was wondering about the who, what, where, when, and why of it. I was, too.

After school I invited everyone from *Real*

News back to my house to view the video. Megan bowed out. Too busy with the popularity patrol.

But the good news was that Tyler invited himself along! He claimed he wanted to check out his camera work.

Maybe, maybe not, right?

Everyone settled around the VCR. I popped in the tape.

"This should be quite interesting," Melody said in her crisp British accent.

Melody is a one-of-a-kind, with a style all her own. Today she wore a skirt that looked like it had been made from strips of black velvet. The hem was pointy and uneven. Her colorful T-shirt was handpainted. I wondered if Melody had made her outfit herself. She sometimes worked on props and scenery for the drama department and was into all things artsy.

She was also into my bud Ringo. I was pretty sure he liked her back. With Ringo, it was hard to tell. He seemed to like everybody.

"Here we are at command central," I heard myself say. The camera jerked across *Real News* headquarters.

"What's with the jittery camera?" Toni complained. "I feel like I'm watching a sequel to the *Blair Witch Project*."

"I was trying to figure out how it worked,"

I protested. "Give me a break."

The footage was less jumpy after Ringo took over in the lunchroom. The problem was, it was deeply strange. "Ringo, you're supposed to keep the camera on the subject," I said.

"I wanted to capture the essence of lunch."

"You did," I said. "Those close-ups of Mystery Stew are the essence of barfdom."

"Brilliant," Melody trilled. This is a popular word in Brit-speak. "I see a future in music video."

At least I could still *hear* the candidates' statements.

When Tyler took over, the tape looked more like a real documentary. Unfortunately, Tyler put the camera on me whenever I asked a question or made a comment. Which was a lot.

I covered my face with my hands. I peered through my fingers. I looked so dorky on TV! And did I really sound like that?

"Way to go, Casey," Toni said. "Scoring excellent points in that election debate."

I snuck a peek at Tyler. Then at the others. No one seemed to be laughing at my video appearance. I uncovered my face.

"You know your way around a camera," Toni said to Tyler. She must have been impressed. Toni is one girl who is pretty stingy with her compliments.

77

"My mom has one," Tyler said. "I've been fooling around with it. I want to learn editing next."

"Can you learn fast?" I asked. "I'm supposed to send this to my mom, but it has far too much realism in it."

I hit the Rewind button.

"You certainly got enough rough material," Melody said. "I don't know how you'll fit it all into a single article."

"I still have to get a statement from Natalie Klein," I realized. "I guess I can just call her. I need to write this up tonight."

"Check this out," Ringo said, pointing at the screen.

"Did we miss something?" I asked. I didn't know if I could sit through watching myself on TV again. It was tough enough the first time.

Ringo had paused the tape on the lunchroom.

"Yeah?" I asked, not getting his point. "So?"

He turned to Tyler. "Can you make this go in slow-mo?"

"I think so," Tyler fiddled with the playback. The video started up again. It was the slow pan I had shot of the lunchroom. Even slower.

"You see?" Ringo said. "All the kids are in groups."

"Of course they're in groups," Toni said. "They're sitting at tables of eight."

"No," Ringo replied. "Like segregated. Like separate and maybe or maybe not equal."

We all stared at the TV. Ringo was right.

There were two tables of black kids. One Latino table; one Asian. Then there was drama club diva Anna Zafrani surrounded by the coolest eighth-grade girls. I spotted the table of sports knuckleheads and the rah-rah squad. Near the windows were the brainiacs. Next to them were the sci-fi freaks. Then the yearbook clique dominated by Spencer Woodham and Willa Greenberg and the other eighth graders who thought they ran the school.

Then there were the stragglers and loners. Jodi. The spiky-haired boy.

Ringo. And behind the camera—me.

Wait a sec, I realized. Ringo has a free transfer between me and the rah-rahs. Which just leaves me.

Great. Video proof of my outsider status. In front of everybody.

"That's an eye-opener," Toni said softly.

"You know, kids would totally freak out if the teachers made us stick to these groups," Ringo said.

"It doesn't seem to be about race," Melody commented. "The athletes are a mixed group. So is the drama club."

"And the brains," Toni added. "But it sure looks as if no one is invited to anyone else's party."

"What's the big surprise?" I demanded. "We all know that Trumbull is just a bunch of cliques ruled by cookie-cutter kids. So what?"

"What about the noncookies?" Melody asked. "What are they supposed to do?"

I looked at her. She was definitely the least cookie of all of us. Except for maybe Ringo. But he was hooked in with the cheerleaders, which gave him an instant ride on the popularity train.

I shrugged. "So what if the groups stick to themselves? Why should it matter?"

"It matters because everyone just sizes each other up without getting to know each other," Tyler said. "And that's not fair. To anybody."

Have I mentioned how smart and sensitive he is?

"And it must be kind of lonely for the kids who don't really fit anywhere," Toni said. Her wistful tone stunned me.

She caught me looking at her. "For the dodos who actually care about that stuff," she added quickly.

Even tough Toni was affected by the popularity bug. How could anyone resist? I wondered how far kids would go to pursue it. Was that why someone had ruined the election posters? Because the election was linked to popularity?

Then I thought back to all the reading I had done about school safety. The media made this big deal over the idea that it was the outsiders, the loners, the nonpopular kids who were most likely to shoot up their classmates.

It had made me mad when I read it. Being a loner doesn't make a person a potential killer. I mean, *I'm* a loner.

It did point up one thing: Popularity is some powerful force.

Would anyone be left standing in its wake?

Girl Reporter Survives Interrogation!

BY THE TIME I got to school Thursday morning, all of the candidates had replaced their ruined posters. Most of the kids seemed to think it was just a prank, and that it was over.

But after all that school safety research, I wasn't too sure. Could this be just the beginning?

I settled into my seat in homeroom. I had just opened up my backpack when a hall monitor came into the room and handed Ms. Wendall a note.

Ms. Wendall glanced up. "Casey? Principal Nachman would like to see you."

My heart thudded. What had I done?

A buzz started up around me. My entire homeroom was wondering the same thing.

No matter how much I grilled the hall monitor,

I got no answer to the big question: What was going on?

As we walked toward the office I spotted Ringo marching toward me, accompanied by his own hall monitor escort. He looked terrified. "Are we in trouble?" he whispered to me.

"I guess," I answered. I glanced at the monitors. Their faces were blank. Like poker players. The bell rang, and they left for class.

"Have a seat please," the principal's secretary said. She got up and went into Principal Nachman's office.

Ringo and I plopped onto the chairs. It was a little too familiar to me. I'd had my share of visits to Principal Nachman's office—and first semester wasn't even over yet.

Another hall monitor entered, followed by the spiky-haired kid from the lunchroom. He was fuming. "This so totally bogus," he complained. "And way typical."

The secretary came back out. "You can go in now," she said.

"Goody," I muttered. Ringo and I meekly filed into Ms. Nachman's office. The spiky-haired boy stormed in after us.

"Hello, Casey," Principal Nachman said. "Let's see. You must be Ringo. And Johnny Ryan."

Is it just me, or is being on a first-name basis

with the principal a bad sign?

"Ms. Nachman," I said, trying to stay calm. "I really think it's unfair that we should be brought down here for questioning without even being told what we did wrong."

"Slow down, Casey." Ms. Nachman said. "You're not under arrest."

"Sure feels like it," Johnny muttered next to me.

Ms. Nachman glared at him, but he just cocked his head to the side. The principal went on, "Mrs. Clemmons, the lunchroom monitor, was disturbed by some things she heard at lunch. Things the three of you were discussing."

"You mean she was eavesdropping?" I asked.

Ms. Nachman tapped a pencil on the table. "Mrs. Clemmons mentioned hearing a rather startling discussion about shooting."

My eyes widened. I was fish-faced speechless. What was she talking about?

Ms. Nachman glared at Johnny, then at Ringo. "She says you each mentioned something about *shooting*?"

Total confusion played across Ringo's face. Then he brightened. He turned to me. "That's right!" he exclaimed, shoving my arm as if it were all a big joke.

Johnny cracked up. He laughed so hard that

he doubled over and clutched his stomach. "Don't you get it?" he said. "Point and shoot."

I hit mental Replay. Lightbulb moment. "Point and shoot," I repeated with a grin.

Johnny was still hooting. "You need to get a little more clued into the lingo," Johnny said to Ms. Nachman.

I couldn't believe this kid. He was talking back to the principal.

"No, *you* need to explain yourself," Ms. Nachman scolded. "Or pack up your books for a nice long suspension and possible criminal charges."

"Whoa!" Johnny held up his hands defensively. "We didn't break any laws. Unless there's a new one about shooting videotape at school."

Ms. Nachman took a deep breath as she finally began to understand. "Videotape?"

I nodded. "I got a video camera so I could make a tape to send to my parents in Asia," I explained. "We were taping some things for them, and I was having trouble with the camera. And they kept saying it's easy, just point and shoot. And—"

Ms. Nachman cut me off. "I get the picture." I squirmed in my seat as she studied the three of us. "Even so, I'd like you three to go talk to Ms. Vermont."

"The guidance counselor?" I stared at her. "But we explained—"

"No argument, Casey. Now go down the hall and wait until Ms. Vermont is ready to see you."

The three of us trooped down the hall to the guidance office. Although I'd dealt with Ms. Vermont before, that didn't make it any easier. The gloomy cloud hanging over us was practically visible. I wondered if there was also a neon "Loser" sign flashing above us.

We trudged into Ms. Vermont's waiting room. Phew. It was empty. Just some chairs, scattered tables piled with pamphlets, and some big plants.

We sat. Far away from the all-too-open hall door.

"At least we're getting out of first period," Johnny said. "Do you think Ms. Vermont is going to call our parents? Because I'm already grounded."

"Ms. Vermont," Ringo repeated. "Vermont. Vermont. I picture trees. Cows. Grass. Ben and Jerry's. This will be fine."

Ms. Vermont opened the door to her office. A girl with tear streaks on her cheeks walked out sniffling.

Johnny stiffened, and Ringo got really pale. I think they were afraid that if they crossed the threshold into Ms. Vermont's office she'd somehow get them to break down and cry. They watched the girl shuffle out of the waiting room.

Ms. Vermont didn't *look* scary. Her brown hair was piled up in a messy bun. She wore a thick green sweater over a long, flowered skirt.

Then I caught a glimpse of her shoes. Converse high-tops! I knew we'd be fine. No grown-up who wore sneakers to school could be all bad. Except maybe for Coach Tickner. But when you teach gym, sneakers aren't optional. Ms. Vermont had chosen those sneakers from an entire world of possible shoes.

Ringo and Johnny stood frozen beside me. "Green," I whispered to Ringo. "She's wearing a green sweater, just like the trees and grass in your visualization. She can't be a monster."

That seemed to relax Ringo. "Uh, here we are, your greenness."

Ms. Vermont looked puzzled, but she smiled. "Come on in."

We stepped into her office. It had a desk and chairs, but everything else looked like a living room or a den. A soft sofa with lots of pillows. A fish tank. Fish.

Ms. Vermont sat behind her desk. We each took a seat in front of her. She gazed at us. She didn't say a word. Not one.

Johnny seemed to want to get the whole thing

over with. "We didn't do anything wrong!" he blurted. "That stupid lunch monitor was eavesdropping and totally misunderstood what we said."

"So you're saying that you feel misunderstood," Ms. Vermont said.

Johnny's face scrunched up like he couldn't believe what he was hearing. His fists clenched on the chair's armrests. "No," he said. "I'm saying that lunchroom lady didn't understand what we said." He sounded like he was talking to a nursery schooler.

Adults are programmed to react to that kind of tone. Badly. I decided I could clear things up without getting us all suspended. "I was using a video camera to do interviews about the election."

Ms. Vermont's face squinched up as if she were listening really, really hard. "Uh-huh. Uh-huh."

I guessed that was my cue to keep talking. "So Ringo and Johnny were giving me pointers about *cameras. Shooting.* Get it? Not guns. Cameras."

I paused so she could get a word in. But she didn't. She just kept her peepers on me, so I kept going. "We had no idea anyone would be eavesdropping. Whatever happened to our constitutional rights? Don't students have the right of free speech anymore?"

Okay, so I got a little loud. Sue me.

"Uh-huh. Uh-huh." Ms. Vermont's murmurs were making me nuts. Why didn't she actually say something?

I guessed I was wrong about the Converse sneakers. That will teach me about judging someone by their appearance.

"Does anyone else have anything they'd like to say?" she asked.

Johnny crossed his arms and glared at the floor.

"I'd like to say 'archipeglio,'" Ringo said. "Only I keep mispronouncing it. Archipeligio. Archpegalo."

"ArkihPELago," Johnny said, sounding it out as if we were hard of hearing.

Ms. Vermont came out from around the desk and perched on its corner. "Now, kids," she said in the kind of voice I imagine doctors use when delivering bad news. "Adjusting to middle school can be difficult. Students who are somewhat less popular sometimes feel latent hostility." She gave us a great big smile. "But I've read your files."

I gasped. "You have files on us? Like the FBI?" Interesting, in a sinister kind of way. I wondered if I could sneak back into this office and get a peek at my file.

"All students have files, Casey. Medical information. Test scores. Transcripts. It helps us keep track of how our students are doing, academically and socially."

This was bizarre. The teachers were keeping tabs on our social lives? Don't they have more important things to do? Like help us prepare for standardized tests and stuff?

"As I was saying," Ms. Vermont continued, "there's nothing in your files to indicate the three of you should have significant problems fitting in. Making friends. Popularity isn't everything, you know."

How come when *I* made that point, it sounded like a totally rational statement, but when she said it, it sounded like an insult?

"I'm sure after this initial period of adjustment all three of you will have no problem making friends and fitting in." She smiled so hard that her cheeks pushed her glasses up a few inches.

Okay, now I was irked. I stood up. "You couldn't *pay* me to be popular," I declared. "I'm proud to be an outsider!"

"Me, too!" Johnny chimed in.

Ringo stared at Ms. Vermont. "You don't think I'm popular?"

The bell rang. We had spent the entire first period being grilled by the administration. Why?

Because we weren't popular. I was furious.

"My door is always open," Ms. Vermont said sweetly. "If any of you feel the need to talk."

"You really think I'm not popular?" Ringo said. He hadn't moved an inch. His gray eyes were like round bowling balls.

I tugged his sleeve. "Come on, Ringo, let's get out of here."

Johnny booked out of there fast. Ringo slowly rose to his feet and shuffled out of Ms. Vermont's office. I guessed he was stunned by the suggestion that he might be less than popular. He was in a daze.

Ms. Vermont's waiting room was now full. Those monitors must be working double time. I wondered if they got bonuses for every kid they dragged in to see a guidance counselor.

I looked around at the waiting kids. I didn't know who they were, but I knew who they weren't. The 'in' clique. Or any clique.

The waiting room was filled with freaks and geeks. The misfits. Not a single one of them would ever be invited to sit at Willa Greenberg's lunch table.

Were all the nonconformists being hauled in for questioning? Were they under surveillance? For what? Being different?

Then I realized that anyone passing the waiting

room would assume Ringo and I were just like the rest of these kids. To the administration, we were. We were all lumped together under a banner saying "Nonclique members."

Just standing here made me feel self-conscious. If someone saw me, they'd think I was a problem child who needed to see the counselor.

I peeked out the door. I had to be sure the coast was clear.

Tyler McKenzie was heading straight toward me.

Male Cheerleader Is So Far Out, He's In!

"OH NO!" I had to hide. I didn't want Tyler to see me in here. What would he think?

I ducked behind Ringo, jumped over three sets of legs and hid behind a chair. Hm. I guess I had some athletic ability after all.

Tyler strolled by without seeing me. Of course, everyone in the waiting room did. Instant weirdo status.

Phew. That was close. Let's try this exit again.

Ringo was still operating in slow-mo, thanks to the vote of no-confidence from Ms. Vermont. I dragged him over to the door and peeked out.

This time, the coast really was clear. No one I knew anywhere.

I pushed Ringo in the direction of his gym class. "Walk," I ordered. "Go. Cheer."

"Yay," he mumbled sadly.

"Forget what Ms. Vermont said," I told him. "I'll see you later."

"Later," he murmured. He vanished into a crowd of kids.

I headed for art class in a hurry. We were making clay sculptures. I couldn't wait to start pounding, smacking, squeezing, and smushing. My hostile feelings were anything but latent.

I had never seen such a crowd in the guidance counselor's office before. Of course, I haven't exactly been keeping tabs. Maybe I should. There might be a story here, too. Or was it all one story: schools threatened by unpopular kids, popularity . . . election?

After school, I slammed into the newsroom. "You won't believe what happened to Ringo and me," I declared as I walked in.

No one was there. Great. I was talking to empty air.

Pounding modeling clay hadn't satisfied me. I had more venting to do. Where was the *Real News* staff? Being interrogated by Ms. Vermont?

"Hi, Casey," Megan said, entering the office. "Do you have your candidates profiles for me already?"

"Not yet," I admitted.

"I hope you're keeping an open mind about Willa," she said.

"I hope you are, too," I replied.

"What do you mean?"

"There *are* other candidates, you know," I said.

"Yeah," Gary said as he strolled in. "What about Natalie?"

"What *about* Natalie?" I asked.

"She's running too, remember."

"I'd rather forget," I said. "Will her first order of business be to hand out Super Soakers to everyone?"

For the last few days Natalie and her swim-team pals had been ambushing boys all over school and drenching them. I was surprised *she* hadn't ended up in Ms. Vermont's office.

Which reminded me. "The weirdest thing happened."

Toni strolled in and tossed a stack of photos onto Dalmatian Station. "What do you think?" she asked. "I snapped some candids of the candidates. I thought they'd be good with the profiles."

"Excellent idea," Megan said.

I put my hands on my hips. "You know, I'm trying to tell you what happened today."

They all ignored me as they gathered around Toni's pictures. "You really captured their person-alities," Megan commented.

If you can't beat 'em, etc. I checked out the pictures. They were great. You could tell these weren't posed.

Dave Tyson perched on the back of his chair with his feet on the seat. An advanced-math textbook lay across his knees. He stared off into space, chewing the end of his pencil. Instead of looking dorky, he looked intense and smart.

Natalie stood at the end of a lunchroom table, arms up as if she was cheering. Her short pixie cut and broad grin made her look excited and friendly.

Jodi Dillard leaned against a wall by one of her flyers, a roll of masking tape on the floor at her feet. She was consulting a schedule. She didn't look lonely, the way she did in the lunchroom. She looked thoughtful, and as if she had a lot of things to do.

Then I came to Willa's photo. Toni must have snapped it just after the bell rang, because kids were filing out of a classroom.

I hated to admit it, but Willa looked like a star. There were other kids around her, but the way Toni took the photo made the other kids blurry. That was kind of how it always was around Willa. Everyone else faded into the background. She was flanked by Stacy Carmel and some of the other popular kids, but she outshone everyone.

"They *are* good," I commented. Then I sighed. "Too bad the only one who has a chance is Willa Greenberg."

"I can't keep track of your opinions, Casey," Megan complained. "One minute you're saying she better watch out. The next minute you're saying the other candidates can't win."

"It's a stupid popularity contest," I said.

"Casey's right," Toni said, backing me up. "There's a whole pecking order in this school, and Willa Greenberg is at the top of the ruling clique."

"Even the teachers buy into all the in-group, out-group junk," I complained.

Ringo shuffled in. He still looked depressed.

Perfect timing. I pointed at him. "Just ask Ringo."

"Just ask Ringo what?" Ringo asked.

"This is what I've been trying to tell you," I said. "Ringo and I, and this kid Johnny Ryan, were all dragged into the principal's office."

"What did you do?" Gary asked.

I glared at him. "That's just it. We didn't do anything!"

"Isn't Johnny that weird guy who dresses all in black?" Megan's brow furrowed as she tried to place him.

"My friend Melody dresses in black," Ringo protested. "She's not weird."

"You see," I said. "You're judging people now by how they dress. That's not fair."

"What happened at the principal's office?" Megan asked.

"We were just *talking* yesterday, by the lunchroom vending machines—and we were totally misinterpreted. Bingo. The next thing you know we're being interrogated. Then she sends us to the guidance counselor. And why? Because we're not the 'popular' kids."

Megan shook her head. "It has to be more than that."

"It wasn't," I snapped. "Do you think if Willa or Spence or you had said 'Point and shoot' any of you would be hauled in and psychoanalyzed? No, of course not. Because you're all such cookie-cutter kids, no one would suspect you were experiencing 'latent hostility'."

"Hm." Toni looked thoughtful.

"What, 'hm'?" I asked.

"That's what the guidance counselor said?" Toni asked. "'Latent hostility'?"

"Yeah, why?"

"My cousin is in high school," she explained. "Kids there are being asked about 'latent hostility,' too. Because of violence in schools. So they're keeping a close eye on kids who are the outsiders, or loner types."

"Like Johnny Ryan," I said softly. Then I thought of something. "They think Ringo and I are that troubled? Just because we don't exactly fit some prototype of the perfect middle-school kid?" I started pacing. I was way bugged.

"That's so unfair," I sputtered. "It makes us suspects in crimes that haven't even been committed. For no other reason than the fact that we're not part of the popular crowd."

Ringo looked stricken. "I never knew I was so out."

I stared at him. It never occurred to me that he'd be so bummed about not being in the popular clique.

He slumped in his chair. I couldn't remember ever seeing him so down. Just because some stupid guidance counselor made him feel unpopular. What kind of guidance was that?

"Listen, Ringo," I said. "You're a *cheerleader*. That's kind of the ultimate definition of popularity."

Ringo lifted his head. "You think?"

"Am I right?" I said to everyone.

"Definitely," Gary said. "Ever since cheerleaders were invented they've been on the top ten list of popularity polls. I'm not exactly sure about guy cheerleaders—"

I whacked Gary's arm.

"But since you're the only one, you're prob- ably double popular," Gary finished. He rubbed the spot where I hit him.

"Gary's right," Megan added. "Cheerleaders are really involved in school spirit. That's what popularity is all about."

I snorted. Megan didn't have a clue.

Girl Reporter Exposes Greedy Girls!

THE NEXT DAY the paper would be put to bed, and I was ready. Almost ready. I had turned in my story about those self-serving politicians, Willa and Stacy. My metal-detector story was on hold until after the PTA meeting. One thing Gram keeps trying to drum into me is not to go to press until you have all the facts. Which is hard to do when you're not exactly the most patient person in the world. But I try.

I needed one more interview to finish the profiles of the candidates. Thursday night, I managed to get hold of Natalie over the phone. What a ditz. It was a good thing I did the interview over the phone. Otherwise I might have been forced to Super Soak her, since she was all wet already.

She did give me an interesting insight into her campaign, however.

"So, Gary," I said, charging into the *Real News* office on Friday morning. "I hear you're the mastermind behind Natalie's run for president."

"She told you that?" he asked. "Since when are you and Natalie tight?"

"We're not," I replied. "I interviewed her for the profile. She said you were the one who suggested she run for president. And why?" I put my finger under my chin and gazed up at the ceiling as if I was thinking really hard. "Let's see, how did she put it? That someone needed to look out for your shared interests."

"You have a problem with that?" he asked me. "You pointed out yourself that the student council makes decisions affecting all the clubs and committees. That means they affect sports, too."

"I take it this means you have your candidates story ready for me?" Megan cut in before I could respond. I could tell she wanted to nip this little tiff before it budded. Okay, we also had a deadline, but that was hours away.

"I have the Brain-Busters story," Gary said, pulling a disk out of his backpack. "They're psyched about getting ready for their first real match next week."

"Here's a story," I teased. "Gary Williams, super-jock, gets into brain games."

"Okay, you win," Gary admitted. "The Brain-Busters team is actually cool. They are primo competitors. They're as hard core about winning as any player on a court or a field. Especially Dave."

"Does this mean you'll be trying out for the next Brain-Busters team?" Megan asked.

I laughed. "Not Gary. He doesn't have a brain to bust."

"Ha ha." Gary said. "So not funny." He wadded up a piece of paper and tossed it at me.

"Will there be enough room in the issue to run Toni's photos?" I asked. "They're so good."

Megan nodded. "I think so. Once Ringo finishes the layout, we'll have a better idea."

"Did someone mention my name?" Ringo walked in. I was glad to see he was back to his cheerful self. "I've got weird news. Bad and good. Is that possible? The bad part is, Angelina Carmichael sprained her ankle yesterday at cheerleading practice. That means I'm on the squad for Saturday's game."

"Good for you, Ringo," I said, patting him on the back.

"So can you come, guys?" he asked. "It's my debut."

"Since I'm on the team, I guess I have no choice," Gary muttered.

I pinged him on the shoulder as Megan and Toni added that they'd be there.

"How about you, Casey?" Ringo asked eagerly.

Spending a Saturday afternoon in a hot, smelly gym was at the bottom of my fun list. But how could I say no to Ringo? "Wouldn't miss it."

"Great!" He lay his sketch book on the table, to show us a new Simon cartoon. "That lunchroom video inspired me."

SIMON SAYS:

EXPRESS YOUR INDIVIDUALITY

Toni laughed. "That is totally on it, Ringo."

"Simon rules," I agreed.

Megan's brow furrowed. "It's great. The only problem is, I don't think we have enough space to run two Simons."

Ringo looked sort of crushed. "That's okay," he said.

"I want to put it in," Megan hurried to say. "But this is our first short issue, and we all have to adjust."

She pulled out her notebook. The pages had curled from Natalie's spraying. Megan squinted to read the splotchy handwriting.

"I really want to run Toni's candids of the candidates. The swim-team portrait will have to wait. We'll use Ringo's 'Mental Gymnastics' cartoon to run with Gary's profile instead. If the swim team wins, we'll run their picture in that issue." She sighed. "But we still have to cut something."

She read and reread her list of stories and pictures.

The whole room held its breath. Even the computers.

Was this it? Was she going to ax my school-funding story? The one that made her brand-new pals look bad?

I chewed the inside of my cheeks to keep myself from blurting out anything.

She tucked a strand of blond hair behind her ear. "Casey's story on the school funding is important. It's in."

Yes! I wanted to raise my fist in the air, but figured this wasn't the time.

"So what's out?" Gary asked.

"If you can tighten up your sports coverage, and we hold off on the new Simon cartoon until next week . . ." She pushed the notebook away. "We'll drop the 'Just Ask Megan' column for this issue."

My jaw dropped. I would never in a million trillion years have given up my own column. My byline would be on two stories this week, and all she'd have was her editorial on the importance of elections.

"Are you sure?" I asked.

She gave me a little smile. "Actually, the letters I was going to answer would go with Ringo's new cartoon. So see, it all works out."

I could tell she was working really hard on being cheerful. Her lips were a little tight, and her voice was chirpy in a weird way.

I was relieved that she was disappointed. It meant she was human. I was beginning to worry.

"We can run two 'JAM's next week," I offered.

Megan gave me an amused look. "I appreciate that, Casey. Especially since you think 'JAM' is wasted column space."

She had me there. Normally I thought that touchy-feely feelings stuff had no place in a hard-hitting newspaper. But I wanted to show Megan support, and I couldn't think of any other way.

"Although I am worried about one thing," Megan added. She sighed. "I don't think Stacy and Willa are going to be very happy with me when this issue comes out Monday morning."

CHAPTER
12

Students Score Big in Superbowl of Smarts!

SATURDAY AFTERNOON I left early for the basketball game. Normally you'd have to threaten to undo my Internet access to get me to show up at a sporting event. But my pal Ringo was cheering in his very first game, and there was no way I was going to miss it.

See? Megan isn't the only one who can be generous. In my book, sitting though a basketball game qualifies as going well above and beyond.

I got to school early so I could check out the Brain-Busters. On Friday Dave had told me they were holding an open practice so the team could get used to playing in front of an audience.

I wasn't the only one who was curious. The room was so crowded I could hardly squeeze inside.

108

The room was covered in charts, lists, maps, math equations. It was as if a deck of flash cards had exploded in there.

Mr. Fitchburg, the advanced-math teacher, stood behind a desk. Five boys and five girls were lined up facing each other.

"All right, the lightning round," Mr. Fitchburg announced. "Teams, send up your players."

Dave Tyson dashed up to Mr. Fitchburg. Some of the boys on his team looked a little bugged. The team of girls conferred, and Patti Ann approached the desk.

Some girls standing near me started chanting: "Go Patti, go Patti."

"Dave'll do it! Dave'll do it," kids shouted from the other side of the room.

My head spun. It was exciting, but it was also weird. These spectators were fired up like this was the superbowl of smarts.

I guess, in a way, it was.

Mr. Fitchburg fired questions at them. "Who was the seventeenth president of the United States? What amendment gave women the vote? What is the atomic number for helium? Which river in North America flows north?"

Dave never let Patti Ann get in a single word. He shouted: "Andrew Johnson, the Nineteenth Amendment, number two and the St. Johns River in Florida." Dave rattled off the answers without a pause for air. The guy was relentless.

"Great job!" Mr. Fitchburg said. "Let's break into new teams."

"I should keep playing," Dave protested. "I won this round. That's how it works on the real show."

"This is practice, Dave," Mr. Fitchburg said. "Everyone gets a chance."

While Mr. Fitchburg flipped through a stack of index cards, the teams rearranged themselves. Some kids sat down, others joined the lineup.

Whoa! I recognized that spiky purple hair! Johnny Ryan was one of the Brain-Busters. Funny, he didn't strike me as a team type.

Oops. There I went, judging a book by its spiky purple cover. I was as bad as the rest of them. On the other hand, I'd gotten a peek at the personality under that spiky purple hair. A little scary.

Hey—and wasn't that Gary? I pushed through a group of admiring Brain-Busters fans and tapped him on the back.

He spun around. "Oh, hi, Casey. It's cool, isn't it?"

"I guess. But aren't you supposed to be on the basketball court?"

Panic crossed his face. "Oh, man!" He dashed

out of there so fast he nearly took half the crowd with him.

I never thought I'd see the day when Gary missed a game because of something that required brains and not brawn.

I watched the practice a little longer. I could kind of see the appeal. It was fast-moving, and you could almost get some of the answers. Almost. Like, you knew that somewhere in your brain was the possibility that the question could be answered, only your brain accessed the info at the speed of a 28.8 modem and the Brain-Busters were fully 56. Maybe higher.

I noticed Dave didn't quite play by the rules. He kept shouting out answers even when it wasn't his turn. Mr. Fitchburg had to reel him in a few times. He was seriously competitive. Made me wonder what kind of student council president he'd be.

I didn't want to miss Ringo's very first official cheer, so I booked out of there.

I pushed open the doors to the gym, perhaps my least favorite location in school. But for some reason the gym is where they insist on playing basketball.

I climbed a few steps into the bleachers and then stopped. I didn't see a single person to sit with. I scanned the stands.

Of course. Megan sat with Willa, Stacy and the rest of that crowd. She kept giggling and smiling. Big surprise. Spence Woodham sat right behind her and kept leaning down to say things to her. Willa and Stacy both looked smug.

Well, I certainly couldn't sit with them. So where should I go? I couldn't just stand here.

A group of girls sitting near me glanced over. Then they huddled together and started whispering.

Are they talking about me? I wondered. Are they making fun of the loser sixth grader who doesn't have any friends?

What is wrong with you? I scolded myself. Why are you worried about what these kids think?

Then I got mad. What was wrong with *them*? Why didn't anyone invite me over? I recognized plenty of these kids from classes. They weren't even *trying* to be friendly. They all acted like I had monster breath.

Get a grip, I told myself. All the talk about popularity lately must have infected my brain.

"Hey, Casey. Looking for someone?" Tyler came up beside me.

I had never been so happy to see anyone in my entire eleven years.

"I was looking for Melody, but I don't see her,"

I fibbed. I didn't want Tyler to think I was hopelessly alone.

"The game's about to begin," he said. "We should grab some seats. We'll save one for her."

I followed Tyler into the bleachers. A smile totally took over my face. Tyler is the most perfect person. He just saved me from being permanently tagged with the big "L."

It was really fun to watch the game with Tyler. We cheered Ringo, which I guess was kind of funny—to cheer the cheerers.

The game ended, and I was honestly disappointed. Not because of the basketball game, which I hadn't followed at all. Because it meant Tyler would leave.

"My mom has a list of chores for me," Tyler said. "So I need to run. Catch you around."

"Yeah, see you." On second thought, I was glad he was in a hurry. I really had to hit the girl's room, and I didn't want him to walk me there.

When I came out of the stall, Megan was primping in the mirror. The perfect opportunity to talk some sense into her.

"I can't believe you're still hanging with those crooked yearbook girls," I declared. Okay, so I jumped right in. I didn't know how long I had—couldn't waste any time on diplomacy.

Megan shook her head. "You don't understand," she protested. "You only know one side of them."

"Well, since they're a pair of cardboard cutouts, that's all I need to know."

"Casey, you don't get it," she said. "They're fun. You know? F-U-N. I kind of can't believe they want to hang out with a sixth grader like me. And fine—I admit it. It's cool to sit with them and have other people notice us. What's wrong with that?"

I stared at her. "What's wrong with that, in case you forgot, is that those girls are the reason you had to cut your 'JAM' column this week."

"It bugs me too, okay? But —"

Willa popped her head into the bathroom. "Megan, we're heading over to Hole-in-the-Mall. Want to come?"

Megan hesitated. Her eyes flicked to me, then back to Willa.

Willa definitely caught the eye action. "Spence is coming," Willa added, dangling him in front of Megan like a catnip toy in front of a kitten.

Megan pounced. "I'll be ready to go in a sec," she promised Willa. Willa smiled and left.

I glared at Megan's reflection in the mirror.

"Casey, try to understand." She lowered her voice as if she were revealing state secrets. "Willa has promised to help me find out if Spence likes me."

"Of course he likes you," I said. Loudly. Just to see her cringe. "Everyone likes you."

"I mean, *likes* me, likes me." Megan said. "I just have to know. Besides," she added as she slid a glittery barrette into her hair, "I want Willa and Stacy to know I'm their friend. Monday's edition of *Real News* is probably going to make them think otherwise."

Megan fluffed up her hair and applied pink lip gloss. She smelled like a strawberry. Then she rushed out of the bathroom in a cloud of pinkness.

Megan was right about one thing. Once Willa and Stacy got their hands on Monday's edition of *Real News*, they might drop Megan like a hot potato.

Who's Hot, Who's Not!

MONDAY MORNING. JUST as I had predicted, *Real News* made a big impact.

I wondered what Willa's and Stacy's reactions would be. The buzz around school was that thanks to my exposé, Willa was no longer a shoo-in.

Kids were also talking about the celebrity profiles, and the questions I'd asked on school safety. This election was going to be more than a popularity contest.

At lunch, I saw Megan picking up ketchup at the condiments counter. I went over.

"Hey, Megan," I said. "Another successful issue."

She gave me a weak smile, then leaned closer to me. "I still haven't seen Willa and Stacy," she whispered. "I'm a little nervous."

"You'll have your chance now," I told her. "Here they come." I was kind of looking forward to seeing their reaction.

Megan fidgeted beside me. She shouldn't have worried. The only one they were mad at was me.

Willa planted herself in front of me. "What did I ever do to you?" she snapped. "Why did you attack me in your stupid newspaper?"

"And me?" Stacy added.

"*A*, the newspaper isn't stupid," I retorted. "And *b*, all I did was report the truth."

To my surprise, Megan backed me up. "Casey checked her facts, and I—"

Willa cut her off. "We don't blame you, Megan," she said. "We know you were only doing your job."

My face felt hot. "What do you think *I* was doing?" I demanded.

Willa's face twisted into a sneer. Amazing how unpretty a pretty girl can get. "You were trying to get back at us."

"For what?" I sneered right back.

"You're jealous." Before I could respond, she hooked her arm through Megan's. "Come on, Megan. Spencer saved us seats." She practically dragged Megan away.

Stacy lingered a moment, glaring at me.

"I am not jealous," I insisted.

"You're going to regret your mean story," Stacy declared. She spun on her heels and followed Megan and Willa.

Mean story? Try true story. I watched them settle at the table. Was Stacy actually threatening me? What could she and Willa possibly do?

I sighed. Nothing had really changed. The popular kids thought they ran things—they even thought they ran me. Then I looked around. I was wrong. Things *had* changed.

Natalie Klein was surrounded by her usual jocks, but now all of them wore "Klein Is Fine" buttons. Jodi Dillard was having an actual conversation with someone. *Real News* just might have had something to do with that. Thanks to Toni's awesome pictures, people finally knew who Jodi was.

But the biggest change: there was a brand-new clique in town. The Brain-Busters team had their own table, and lots of the other kids were jockeying for their attention. Dave Tyson was at the center of it all, smiling, talking.

Wow. Geek was now in.

Johnny Ryan waved at me from the Brain-Busters table. I guess he felt we were friends since we'd shared a bonding moment. Nothing like an interrogation to bring kids together.

I waved back, smiling. I wondered what Ms.

Vermont would think of Johnny's new status as a member of the Brain clique.

And here I was again—all by myself. This was getting ridiculous. I felt as if I wore an "Uncool" sign on my chest.

Stop harping on it, I ordered myself. I shook my head. Must have been Stacy's threat that made me self-conscious.

Despite my allergy to the rah-rah squad, I walked right over to the cheerleader table. I needed a dose of Ringo reality.

"Case," Ringo greeted me. "Sit. Munch. Chill."

"Wasn't Ringo's 'mental gymnastics' cartoon cute?" a blond girl with two bouncing ponytails chirped.

"I thought it was *gross!*" But the way the girl giggled made it dead obvious she liked it.

A girl with an Ace bandage on her ankle hobbled over on crutches. "Didn't Ringo cheer a great game?" she asked, easing into the chair beside me. I figured this was Angelina Carmichael, the reason for Ringo's debut on Saturday. "I wish I could have cheered, but he did a great job."

"I'm trying to come up with a cheer you can do standing on one leg," Ringo said. "We'll have one ready for the next game."

"That's so awesome," Angelina gushed.

All this cheeriness didn't exactly cheer me. I

felt like an outsider. I wasn't part of their group, either.

So what group did I belong to?

I stopped thinking about the in-group/ out-group/Casey no-group problem once I hit Dalmatian Station. This week's story meeting went quickly. We would run Megan's missed "JAM" column, Ringo's individuality cartoon, Gary's sports coverage, my story on school safety and, of course, the election results. The vote would be on Thursday, so we shouldn't have any trouble getting everything in for the Friday layout.

The meeting over, Gary, Ringo and I decided to check out the Brain-Busters practice. Again, Ringo wanted to volunteer his services as cheer- leader.

The practice was a standing-room-only event. It's possible that there were even more kids there than on Saturday.

"Hi, guys," Gary called to some of his friends. "Isn't it awesome?" he said to me. "This team really rocks."

I scanned the room. Amazing. Three of Gary's jock buddies were there, in uniform. They must have snuck away from practice to be here. Some- how brainisms beat out balls, hoops and sticks. I spotted a tall, gangly basketball dude studying nded on it.

asked.

an alternate universe—
...sy-turvy. In this world,
frou-frous looked up
't remember leaving

...s became the major players at
was next? Megan going grunge?
As much as I hated to admit it, cliques
...eotypes made life predictable—and re-
...ng.

...spotted Natalie and Jodi sitting at the back of
...e room. Willa's clones, Stacy and Katherine,
stood by the door.

Were they here to watch practice, I wondered,
or check out the election competition?

I studied Dave as his team went into the lightning round. He practically foamed at the mouth,
pushing the players faster, harder. He got really
mad if a teammate lost a point, and was always
cutting in. In fact, Mr. Fitchburg had to tell him
to ease up.

"But I want us to win," Dave protested. "If I
know the answer, shouldn't I do all I can to win
the game?"

"Sportsmanship counts on this team, too," Mr.
Fitchburg reminded him.

Dave looked annoyed. "But—"

"Sit down, Dave. We all know you[...]
this. Others need a shot."

Dave started to protest, then shut his[...]
He sat down. His face said it all. He wa[...]
much not pleased.

Dave definitely played to win.

I wondered if that was true of his camp[...]
as well.

CHAPTER 14

News Staff Lost in Crush Kingdom!

TUESDAY MORNING AT school the first person I saw was Dave. It seemed like he had been waiting for me.

"Casey, there's something I want to show you," he said.

I followed him into the building. He stood me in front of the row of campaign posters.

"Okay . . ." I said, not getting what he was trying to show me. "The slogans are a little weak, but—"

"Look closely," he instructed. "What do you see? I mean, what *don't* you see?"

Then it hit me. "You! I don't see you. Your big poster is gone."

"Actually," he said, "They're all gone. I

checked." He shook his head. "Last week someone ruins the posters. Now they steal them. What gives?"

"Someone is sabotaging the election," I declared. My nose tingled just the way I like it. This was turning into an actual news story.

Okay, think, I told myself as I sat in history class. What does this person have to gain by first destroying all the posters and then getting rid of Dave's? It doesn't add up.

I was a total space case all day. I made Ringo look linear. My mind kept going round and round in the Terminator's math class. I had more important things on my mind than square roots and exponents. I had an investigation to conduct!

I tried to think about each piece of the puzzle. The vandalism seemed like a prank. The stolen posters changed everything. What was the culprit after? Was he—or she—hoping to draw attention to the candidates whose posters were left on the walls? Or did this action actually bring Dave more attention—and was that the intention?

I hit the *Real News* office after school with energy to spare. Megan seemed even more excited than me.

Rats. She was talking about Stacy and Willa.

"They promised to invite Spence along whenever we get together," Megan was confiding to

Toni. "And don't you just love this skirt?" The girl actually twirled. I thought I'd puke. "Willa picked it out for me at the mall. I never would have had the nerve to put these colors together, but they totally work, don't you think?"

"You got it goin' on," Toni agreed. "You look awesome."

"It's really fun hanging out with Stacy and Willa," Megan gushed.

"This is not about fun. This is a newspaper office, and I have a story to cover," I declared.

It was as if Megan couldn't hear me. Was I speaking in a frequency only dogs could hear?

"Maybe if I knew one way or the other about Spencer, I could stop obsessing," Megan said. "If he's not interested, I can just get on with my life."

As if. "Megan," I said. "Please return from Crush Kingdom long enough to discuss an important news story."

Megan sighed. "Okay, what?"

"What do you mean, what?" I said. "Haven't you noticed what's been going on? Or are you too caught up in fluff to see anything unless Willa or Spence points it out to you?"

Megan looked confused. "What are you talking about?"

"Hello? We're talking vandalism. Crimes against

the candidates. Election scandal. Someone is sabotaging the school elections. I'd think you'd have noticed since your new best friend happens to be running."

And is a prime suspect, I added silently.

"It is kind of weird," Toni said. "One day no one cares about the election, now it's all they talk about."

I looked around the table. "But this is getting scary. If they targeted Dave, where will they stop? And who do we think did it?"

"Don't get ahead of yourself, Casey," Megan cautioned. "Just report the facts. No wild accusations."

"Of course not!" I said indignantly. "But I don't have a lot of time to gather those facts. It's already Tuesday. The debates are tomorrow. The big vote is Thursday. This is going to be a front-page story on Monday morning—*if* I can get some help."

"Count me in," Gary said.

"Me, too," Toni chimed in.

"Me, three," Ringo said.

We all looked at Megan. "I can't," she said. "You said it yourself. One of my friends is running. I have to stay out of it."

"Especially since Willa tops my suspect list," I muttered. Okay, so I said it loud enough for her to hear me.

Megan's eyes widened. "How can you say that?"

I shrugged. "Her poster wasn't torn down."

"She wouldn't need to stoop to such pranks," Megan said. "She's already popular. Everyone knows her. And most people like her."

"She probably thought this election was going to be a breeze," I said. "Then the Brain-Busters got hot, and suddenly Dave is a real threat."

"He's a threat to Natalie and Jodi," Toni pointed out.

"Nat's my friend and everything," Gary said, "But she and Jodi are lagging way behind. That could make them a little desperate. But I definitely don't see Natalie as the type," he added firmly.

"Could Dave have torn down his own poster?" Toni asked. "I know it would be kind of a weird thing to do, but it might get him the sympathy vote."

"It sure got everyone talking about him," Ringo said.

"And he's really competitive," Gary added.

I nodded. "I've seen him in action." I drummed my fingers on the polka-dot table. "We have our work cut out for us. If we don't get to the bottom of this, the culprit could wind up getting elected!"

"So how do you think we should start?" Ringo asked.

I narrowed my eyes, thinking. "Whoever stole the posters tore down a lot of them. We have to figure out who could have done it, and where they dumped them."

Mr. Baxter hurried in. He carried his briefcase and a note. "Casey, Ringo, I have a message here that you two are to go to Ms. Vermont's office."

Ringo and I stared at him.

Now what?

Swimmer Forced to Take
Her Last Spritz!

It took me a minute to process. "What does she want now?"

Mr. Baxter shrugged. "The note doesn't explain why Ms. Vermont wants to see you two. Just when. Now."

I packed up my stuff. Ringo slowly gathered his belongings. I wasn't going to let this little setback interfere with the investigation.

I looked at Gary and Toni. "You guys get started, okay?"

They both nodded. "We'll check Dumpsters to try to figure out where they tossed them," Gary said. "That might give us some clues."

"Excellent," I said. "Remember, we have to find out both motive and opportunity. That's the key to getting to the bottom of a case."

"Good thinking," Mr. Baxter said. "But now you and Ringo need to get to the bottom of the mystery in Ms. Vermont's office."

Megan was noticeably silent. She was probably worrying how her popularity would be affected by fraternizing with known weirdos.

Ringo and I trudged to Ms. Vermont's office. As we passed the front entrance my eyes bugged. Some hefty guys were setting up a metal detector. Ms. Caldwell, the PTA president, was overseeing everything.

"Hold on," I told Ringo. Ms. Vermont would have to wait. I had to find out what was going on.

"Excuse me?" I said. Whoa. Gram was right. Ms. Caldwell's hairspray was seriously potent. "I thought you weren't going to install the metal detectors until after the PTA meeting this week."

Ms. Caldwell squinted down at me. "You're that Casey Smith, aren't you?"

Wow. I'm famous. Only the way she said my name didn't make it sound like a compliment.

"Yes," I admitted. "Gram has mentioned you to me, too," I added, with a fake sweet smile.

"Well, Casey, we thought we'd jump-start the process by putting in one detector. That way we can make sure they work."

She jumped when the alarms started going off

behind her. "Are they supposed to do that?" I asked.

Her eyes narrowed into a glare.

Ringo tugged my arm. "Casey, let's go. I don't want to get into more trouble."

Reluctantly, I turned away from Ms. Caldwell. And headed toward the office of another bothersome grown-up—Ms. Vermont.

Where we got another surprise.

Who was just leaving Ms. Vermont's waiting room?

Natalie Klein.

She didn't look upset, though.

"What are you doing here?" Ringo asked.

"They confiscated my Super Soaker," Natalie explained. "Ms. Vermont thought I had some deep-seated problem with boys, since I didn't soak any girls." Natalie giggled. "I explained the dare was very clear. Spray boys. If someone dared me to spray plants, I would have done that. I guess she decided I didn't have any latent feelings of hostility."

Natalie giggled again and left. I stared after her. She didn't know it, but she had just answered a big question. And Super Soakers were the answer.

That's how the posters were ruined. Someone had sprayed them with water. I remembered how Megan's notebook had looked after Natalie ambushed Gary. The ink had run all together. Just like the posters.

Did Natalie spray the campaign posters? But why would she do that? Then it hit me—what if it was an accident? Maybe some boy target had been standing in front of the posters when Natalie let loose. Then she was too afraid of getting into trouble to admit it.

Then maybe, I thought, the wheels turning, maybe accidentally ruining the posters gave her the idea to tear down Dave's.

Still, Natalie just didn't strike me as the type. But I was learning that looks can be deceiving.

Johnny Ryan showed up while Ringo and I waited to see Ms. Vermont. "You, too?" he asked.

"They must think we're some kind of Three Musketeers or something," I said.

"My dad always wanted to be a Mouseketeer," Ringo said. "So I got him a hat with mouse ears for his birthday."

Ms. Vermont opened her door. Today she looked like a big bunny rabbit. Her sweater was white and fluffy, her skirt was blue and fluffy. I glanced down at her shoes. I half expected to see her wearing fuzzy bunny slippers, but she wore baby-blue high-tops.

I need to rethink my shoe wardrobe. I didn't

like the idea I was wearing the same shoes as this phony.

We filed into the room and sat down. Ms. Vermont leaned against the front of her desk and smiled at us. None of us were fooled.

Johnny stared at his feet. Ringo braced for bad news. I think he was worried she'd tell him he wasn't popular again.

"I'm sure you know why you're here," she announced.

We all stared blankly at Ms. Vermont. She sighed.

"As you know, there has been some vandalism in our school."

My heart started to thump. Did she think we're the ones responsible? Were we being accused?

"It's terrible, don't you think?" Ringo asked.

"I'd like to have a better sense of what *you* think," Ms. Vermont said.

"I think the whole millennium issue is confusing," Ringo said. "Did the millennium begin in 2000, or will it be in 2001? And Chinese New Year is on a different day. Is it the millennium in China, too?"

Ms. Vermont took a deep breath. "Let's stay on the subject at hand."

She was no match for Ringo logic.

"What *is* the subject at hand?" I asked. "We don't know why we're here."

"You three have expressed some rather strong views regarding the election," she replied. "Campaign posters were damaged, and some have now disappeared."

"You think we did it?" I screeched. I hit Pause and lowered my volume. "I mean, do you think we're the ones responsible?"

"We're just trying to get to the bottom of this unfortunate incident." She stared at me as if she was trying to search deep into my soul. My soul was none of her business.

"All we did was express our opinions, and suddenly we're suspects?" I was outraged. "Have people been spying on us? Whatever happened to free speech?"

Ringo looked horrified. "I would never have destroyed those posters. Each time, the candidates had to make more. That meant more trees had to die. And I'm on the side of keeping as many trees alive as possible."

I could see Ms. Vermont trying to figure out if Ringo was for real or not. I decided to help her out. "He totally means that," I said. "Just check out his Simon cartoons in *Real News* and you'll get on the Ringo wavelength."

Her eyes focused on me. My face grew hot again, from both scrutiny and indignation. "You are so off base," I told her. "Why would I destroy the posters? I'm the one who got the kids interested in the election in the first place. Until my story came out, all the kids were as apathetic as Johnny here."

Oops. I glanced over at him. "Sorry, Johnny."

He shrugged. "No sweat. I mean, like Casey says, I think the election is bogus. Why would I bother trying to sabotage it? It's not worth my time. I don't care who wins. I don't care who loses. They're all pretty drippy in my book."

Ms. Vermont's eyes darted from my face, to Ringo's, then Johnny's and then back to mine again. "I believe you three are telling me the truth."

"Can we go?" Johnny asked. "I don't want to be late for my Brain-Busters practice." He slung his big backpack over one shoulder.

"I have to get to cheerleading practice," Ringo added.

"And I have a story to write," I said. "You know, next time you haul us in, could you do it? I'd love to skate out of gym class."

Ms. Vermont frowned, as if she was trying to figure out an excuse to keep grilling us, but couldn't. "Run along," she said. "Just remember, vandalism is usually the work of a child in trouble. Please, if you know anyone like that, urge them to come see me."

"Yeah, sure," Johnny muttered.

We filed out of the office. "I think I'll tag along with Johnny," I told Ringo. "I have some questions I want to ask Dave."

"Ask him about the millennium thing. He should know."

Johnny and I headed for the Brain-Busters practice. My brain clicked away, ticking off questions.

Was Dave a suspect? Only an interview would tell me for sure. Luckily, the Brain-Busters had already done so much brain-busting that they were taking a break. Johnny got razzed over being late, but he explained about Ms. Vermont, and I was his alibi.

That got me started off on a good foot with Dave.

"She really thought you could have had something to do with it?" he asked, incredulous. "She's the one who needs counseling."

"She thinks whoever did it might be troubled," I explained. "I think she's missing the point. I think whoever did it has something to gain."

"But what?" Dave asked. "What's the fun of winning if you don't do it fair and square? It makes the win a whole lot less satisfying."

"You have a point." I only wondered if he meant it. I knew how competitive he was.

But would he really have accomplished anything by Super Soaking the posters and then tearing down his own?

Then it hit me. *Ping*. The only way the incidents made sense was if they were done by two different people. For completely different reasons.

So maybe I was right. Natalie could have accidentally destroyed the posters.

Watching Johnny Ryan gave me a different idea. Maybe it wasn't an accident at all. Maybe the vandalism was an expression of an opinion. A prank demonstrating someone's feelings toward the whole school election thing.

Someone who thought the whole school election thing was just bogus. Drippy.

Someone like Johnny, who had just pulled a Super Soaker out of his oversized backpack.

Elections Labeled "Drippy!"

JOHNNY TIPPED HIS head back and drank from his blue Super Soaker.

I strode up behind him and tapped him on the shoulder. "I guess answering all those questions made you thirsty."

He wiped his mouth on his sleeve. "Uh-huh."

"Do you always carry that Super Soaker around?"

"Yeah," he said. "It's a lot cooler than the designer water bottles the jocks carry."

"Comes in handy when you want to ruin a row of posters, doesn't it."

Johnny stared at me as if I had grown a second head. I hoped it didn't have the same hairstyle as his.

"Come on, Johnny," I insisted. "I know you did

it." I didn't really, but I had one wicked hunch. Gram always says a good reporter has excellent instincts.

Johnny's eyes narrowed, then he smiled at me. "Maybe I did, maybe I didn't. So what? They're all drips, anyway."

"Even your teammate Dave?" I asked.

Johnny shrugged. "Dave's a good player, but I don't get this whole school president thing. Total dorkiness."

"Is that why you tore down his posters?" I demanded.

"Whoa. Slow down, Snoopy. I didn't touch his stupid posters."

"Why should I believe you?"

"Look, I think the whole election bag is one big bogus exercise in dumbness," he said. "I don't care who wins."

I stared at him really hard, hoping something would tell me if he was telling me the truth. Come on, instincts. Kick in.

"Johnny! We're up," Dave called.

"I've gotta get back into the game," Johnny took another gulp from his Super Soaker and charged to the front of the room.

Gr. No confession. No evidence. No proof.

Ringo popped his head into the room. "There you are."

I hurried over to him. We huddled in the corridor. "Did you find out anything?"

"I talked to the janitor," Ringo reported. "He's really nice. Did you know that club soda is a good stain remover?"

"Focus, Ringo."

"Oh, yeah. Trash pickup was last night," he informed me. "So if the posters were torn down after school yesterday, they'd be gone by now."

I slumped against the wall. "So there goes our evidence."

"Hey!" Gary said. He and Toni dashed down the hall toward us. "Look what we found."

He and Toni held up some torn and crumpled posters.

"Where did you find them?" I asked.

"In the Dumpster near the side entrance," Toni said. "Girl, I do not ever want to search through school garbage again. There are some serious pigs in this school."

"That's weird." I stared at the messy posters.

"That middle-school kids are gross?" Gary said. "What's weird about that?"

I made a face at Gary. "No. That means the posters were torn down early this morning. And whoever did it carried them all the way over to the other side of the school to toss them. Why would they risk getting caught by carrying them through the halls?"

"They could have carried them in a backpack or something," Gary pointed out. "We just have to find out who has something like that."

"That's, like, everybody," Toni said. "It doesn't exactly narrow things down."

"Maybe whoever did it had a class on that side of school," I said. "They had just enough time to rip down the posters, run over to the side entrance and then get to class."

"Makes sense," Gary said.

"So who would be over on that side of the school?" I asked. "And who would have access to the building before school?"

Gary's eyes dropped to the ground. "Athletes," he mumbled. Then he gazed defiantly at me. "But I don't think Natalie had anything to do with this. I know she has a Super Soaker and everything . . ." He trailed off.

"One of her friends could have done it for her," Toni pointed out. "Even without her knowing. A lot of the guys think she's really cute."

"Jock guys, who could have been here for early morning drills," I said.

"I think you're way off base," Gary complained.

141

"Prove me wrong," I told him. "Help me figure out who did it."

"That weird Jodi person," Gary suggested.

"She might have motive. But did she have opportunity?"

"A lot of clubs meet before school," Gary reminded us.

"I don't think she belongs to any clubs," I said.

"There are sixth-grade homerooms over there," Ringo said. "We should find out which homeroom she's in."

"Willa was probably at a yearbook meeting," I added. "I think Megan said she was. And Dave was here for Brain-Busters. Then there's the question of whether Johnny was really telling the truth or not."

We all stared at each other.

Everyone was still a suspect.

Metal Detectors Turn School into Jail!

ON WEDNESDAY MORNING I had my first walk through the school metal detectors. Gave me a really creepy feeling. My whole body tensed up. Which was so bogus—I knew I didn't have anything hidden in my backpack or pockets, and I still felt guilty.

I wondered if everyone else felt the same way.

It took forever to get into school. The stupid machine kept going off. Then kids would have to empty out their pockets and try again. And again. Finally the security guards gave up and let everyone through.

Man. Instead of being a serious tool for security, the metal detector was a major joke.

I finally made it to my locker. My eyes widened as I read a typed note that was taped to it.

```
Jodi Dillard=JODI DULL-ARD!
Don't vote for her for student
        council president.
```

I looked at the locker next to mine. This note was different. It said:

```
Katherine CUTTER doesn't CUT IT.
    Don't vote for her for
      seventh-grade rep.
```

I scanned the hall. Notes were taped to most of the lockers. It seemed that only Jodi and Katherine were the targets this time.

Things were really heating up. Why was the election so important? This wasn't about doing the right thing for the student body anymore. This was about something else. Power? Attention?

It also seemed extreme. Irrational, even. And it made me wonder how far this culprit would be willing to go. Were there kids at Trumbull who were really troubled? Like the kids at those other schools where the shootings took place?

Between the metal detector and the notes, the entire school was majorly buzzing. As soon as I slid into my chair in homeroom I made a list of suspects.

<u>Dave</u>: Loves to win. Cares about the election. Cares too much? He's smart enough to carry out any plan.

<u>Willa</u>: Losing would be humiliating for the popularity princess. Thought she'd win without a problem. Trying to regain her position at the top of the polls?

Something wasn't right here. Katherine Cutter was part of the Willa Trio. She followed Willa around like a puppy, and Willa treated her like a personal servant. I could see why Katherine might get fed up with Willa, but Willa had a good deal going with Katherine. She wouldn't try to sabotage Katherine's election. She probably wanted to fill the student council with all her friends.

Unless she slammed Katherine to throw suspicion off her. Which could also explain Dave's missing poster. He could have thought the same thing and torn down his own posters. Would that explain Jodi?

<u>Jodi</u>: A big unknown. Needs this election so that someone might finally notice her.

145

Saw Dave as main rival. (tore down posters?) But—would she stick up notes about herself?

Natalie: Hasn't seemed very interested in the election since the first day. A cover?

Was at Brain-Busters—checking out the competition? Could one of her jock friends be behind it without her knowing it?

I knew I'd only make myself crazy if I included all the reps as potential suspects. Besides, it really was mostly the presidential candidates who had been targeted. Willa and Natalie were the only ones left alone. And one of Willa's friends had just been dissed. That left Natalie, either because she was the culprit or because no one viewed her as a threat.

I needed to interview these suspects. I needed to try to catch them in the act. But how? I had no idea when or how the culprit would strike.

"Attention, students!" Principal Nachman's voice blared from the loudspeaker. "Please bear with us as we test the metal detector. I am counting on you to be patient."

She cleared her throat. It wasn't a pretty sound over a loudspeaker. "Due to recent events surrounding the election," she continued, "you are all on notice. If there is one more incident, the election will be canceled. You will not be allowed to participate in student government if you don't have the necessary maturity or responsibility. Democracy is a privilege. Don't make us regret we've granted it to you."

Granted it to you? Excuse me?

I pulled out my notebook and wrote:

Work on "democracy" editorial.

Then I added another name.

<u>Johnny Ryan</u>: Thinks the election is stupid. Did he want to get it canceled all along?

Would the suspect pull back, now that the election was threatened? After all, if there was no election, there would be no student government to run. I really needed to get to the bottom of this. This story was even more interesting than I first thought. I just hoped Ringo, Johnny and I weren't rounded up again before it was all over.

* * *

After homeroom I had to make a pit stop in the girls' bathroom. While I was washing my hands I heard a weird noise, like a whimper.

I turned off the water. I heard the sound again. I knew what it was—crying.

I checked the row of stalls. No feet.

Should I say something? The girl must be sitting on a seat with her knees pulled up. That meant she didn't want anyone to see her.

I decided I would just sneak out. If I was having a breakdown at school I wouldn't want anyone to see me either. The Constitution implies that everybody has a Right to Privacy. I figured the bathroom was definitely a Right to Privacy zone.

But then the bell rang. The girl's loafers hit the tile floor, and she yanked open the stall door.

Jodi Dillard's tear-streaked face was inches away from mine.

"Uh, sorry," I muttered. "I wasn't spying. I was . . ."

Jodi looked down.

"Uh, are you okay?" Sensitivity isn't my strong suit. I thought that was a pretty good opening.

Jodi's shoulders shook. Great. I just made her start crying all over again.

"I didn't mean to upset you," I said.

"It's not you," Jodi said. "It's this." She held a crumpled piece of paper out to me.

I took it. It was one of the notes plastered all over the lockers. The one that said "Jodi Dillard = Jodi DULL-ARD."

I didn't know what to say. I've had kids mad at me, and I've gotten into fights and stuff, but I've never had a nasty note about me posted all over school.

"This is really mean," I said.

Jodi's eyes filled with tears again. "Why would someone do this? I can't help it if I'm boring."

"You know, they did the same thing to Katherine Cutter," I pointed out. I hoped that would make her feel better. That it wasn't just her being picked on. "It's because of the election."

"I wish I had never decided to run for student council president," she said. She strode over to the sink and splashed water on her face. "I don't know what I was thinking."

"Why did you run?" It was something I was curious about. She wasn't the usual candidate. She came out of nowhere and was such a long shot.

Jodi's face crumpled again. "I thought . . . it seemed like . . . " She took a deep breath. "I was so sick of being invisible," she wailed. She burst into tears again.

I didn't know what to do. This was much more Megan's area.

I went into a stall and yanked some toilet tissue from the roll. I handed it to Jodi.

She took it and blew her nose. "I've gone to school here for two years, and hardly anyone knows who I am—just the teachers, because I have such high scores."

"Why didn't you join Brain-Busters?" I asked. "That's for whiz kids, and it seems to be an instant popularity booster."

Jodi shuddered. "Go on TV? No way. It's way too much pressure for me."

"What about other clubs?"

Jodi shrugged. "I always had to baby-sit after school. I couldn't do any after-school activities. But now there's day care at my mom's job. This was the first time I could join anything. Running for president seemed like the quickest route to get somewhere."

So even Jodi saw the election as a ticket to popularity. Depressing.

"Now it all seems like a horrible mistake," she wailed. "Everyone's going to think even worse of me than they did before. If they thought of me at all."

"No they won't," I assured her. "Kids know

that only one person can win an election. They don't hold it against the loser. I mean," I added hastily, "the one who didn't win."

"I wish I had never started this whole stupid campaign." Her voice shook a little. I really hoped she wouldn't start crying again. "But it's too late to back out now."

The second bell rang.

"Oh no!" Jodi gasped. "We're going to be late. I've never been late to class."

Never been late? I'm pretty sure I've made it to class before the late bell rang exactly once.

Jodi splashed cold water on her face. I pulled a whole wad of paper towels out of the holder and handed them to her. Her eyes were kind of red, but the water had put her face back to normal. She raced out of the bathroom so fast she was a beige blur.

I dashed up the stairs to math class. I felt bad for Jodi. Whoever the culprit was had really hurt her feelings.

But she was desperate to win. Actually, I think she was more desperate not to lose than she was to win. That could push her to destroy Dave's posters. She saw him as her main competition.

On the other hand, she sure hadn't put up

those notes. Jodi was more into rules than Megan—and Megan follows rules that haven't even made it into the rule book yet.

Could the culprit be hoping Jodi would drop out of the race? But who would seriously consider her a contender?

Dave. He'd be afraid they'd split the smartie vote and the election would go to Willa.

Then again, what if they were *all* guilty? What if the notes were retaliation against the torn posters? Even if Johnny Ryan sprayed the posters as a prank, one of the candidates could have thought a competitor did it and was trying to get revenge. Each thing could have been done by a different person.

Okay. My head was officially about to explode.

I needed a dose of Griffin. Luckily, I had a study period after lunch, so I just had to get through a couple more classes. Then I zipped over to the computer lab and logged on.

We weren't supposed to use the school computers for our personal stuff, but this was an emergency. Besides, I was trying to gain perspective so I could write a balanced news story.

Yeah. That'll fly, I thought. I wonder if it's a good thing that I think up my alibis before I get caught.

To: Thebeast
From: Wordpainter
Re: The whole world is whacked
   This place has gone completely crazy. Kids are so desperate for popularity that the election is being sabotaged.

I went on to describe my bathroom conference with Jodi and filled Grif in on the election scramble.

   Am I the only one who cares about more important things than who's in and who's out?

I was shocked when Griffin instant-messaged me back. I figured he wouldn't write me until after school. Was he online in his school library, too?

To: Wordpainter
From: Thebeast
Re: The pain of popularity
   Believe me, you're not alone. Wanting to be popular makes kids do the weirdest things. But I'm surprised you don't see why it matters. We all want to fit in somewhere. Even you.
   G

Before I wailed on Griffin for lumping me with all of the rest of the shallow popularity seekers, I had to ask him a question.

Where are you? How'd you get my message?

His reply:

I'm home with the wicked flu. If I don't instant-message you back, it's because I'm puking my guts out.

To: Thebeast
From: Wordpainter
Re: GROSS!!!!!!!!!!!!!!!!!!
  Dear Griffin:
  Too much information!

I hit Send. While I waited for a message back, I flashed back to when I couldn't find anyone to sit with at the game. And when I realized everyone had a group to hang with at lunch except me. I pushed aside those thoughts. They were momentary brain freezes, that's all. Not my usual MO at all.

Griffin took a while, so I wondered if he was throwing up. Finally, he came back on and we went into a private chat.

G: You want to win the Pulitzer prize, right?

C: Why the change of subject?

G: It's not. Go with me on this. Why do you want to win the Pulitzer prize?

C: Has the flu affected your brain cells? It's the highest honor in journalism.

G: And would send you to the head of your class (like student council president) and make you popular among your peers. They'd even envy you, maybe.

C: The Pulitzer is NOT A POPULARITY CONTEST (AND I MEAN ALL THESE CAPITAL LETTERS!) IT IS BASED ON MERIT! TALENT! SKILL! INTEGRITY!

G: QUIT YELLING AT ME! I'M SICK! Why do you need a prize for all of that? Isn't the work enough? Besides, a kid never won the Pulitzer.

C: Not yet!

I wrinkled my nose and stared at the screen. That last question stumped me. I mean, I know the work is supposed to be what matters. But a prize would be nice, too. How could I explain that in a way that made sense, so I didn't sound shallow?

Griffin must have sensed my pause.

G: How about if I answer for you: Validation. The prize is proof that you're doing well, on the right track, good at what you do—all that stuff. For some kids, being popular is all they have. That's how they know they're not total losers—they're okay.

C: Who are you and what have you done with my friend Griffin?

G: Okay, I confess. There's a talk show on TV and today's subject is self-esteem.

C: Cheater! I suspected you were channeling Oprah Winfrey all along. But I do get your point.

G: Good. I have to go now. Sitting up is having a really bad effect on me.

C: Feel better!!

Griffin got me thinking. It must be scary to want to be popular just for being popular. There's so much more at stake that way.

Sure, I want to be admired for being a good journalist, but that's something I can work on. Between Gram and Megan I can't get away with sloppy writing, and I'm getting better all the time. At the rate I'm going, I should be pretty awesome by the time I'm a grown-up. In the meantime, it felt good to have kids read my stories and respond. Sometimes the stories got me in trouble, and sometimes kids disagreed, but most kids knew who I was and what mattered to me. I was getting my thoughts out there, and it kind of gave me a hook. Journalism was what I was known for . . . who I was.

But what about a kid who only had likability? I'd be a total flop! My mouth had a habit of working before my brain kicked in, so I've been known to rub people the wrong way. Living your life to be liked—that would be some amazing pressure.

I thought back to the research I'd been doing on school safety. One survey said that 40 percent of kids surveyed thought that school violence was caused by poor peer relations. I took that to mean not fitting in, being seen as an outsider. In other words, seriously lacking in popularity.

I shivered. It made me sad to think that really troubled kids would care so much about cliques and popularity that it would make them do such terrible things.

Then I got angry. It shouldn't be this important! Another survey found that most kids would rather be popular than smart. I just wanted to shout at them: GET REAL! Who's in and who's out changes daily. Check out movie stars. Last week's hottest sensation is a total nobody this week. And by next week someone new will be on top, and then back at the bottom, in the not-too-distant future.

Then I thought of Jodi and got sad all over again. This was a real problem that wasn't going to go away. She was hurting. And whoever planted those notes was hurting too—just in some other way. All because this stupid election mattered so much to them.

I also understood why Ms. Nachman and Ms. Vermont were so jumpy and hyperaware. I guess they had to be, with the kind of problems schools were confronted by.

But weren't they adding to the problem by tagging certain kids as potential problems? If someone was already feeling like an outsider, being questioned by the guidance counselor could be just the thing to push a troubled kid over the edge. It was like stamping "Loser" across their forehead. Like that would really help a kid fit in.

Wait a second! That was exactly what happened to me, Ringo and Johnny. Were we going to be constantly scrutinized as potential troublemakers? Violent kids? Man. That would make this a really long three years of school.

The bell rang. I bumped into Melody on the way out of the library.

"Cheers," she said.

"Isn't that what you say before you clink glasses?" I asked.

"Actually, it's something of an all-purpose expression in England," she explained. "Have you heard the latest?"

"No. What?" Had the election saboteur struck again? Darn, I really wished I could catch them in the act.

"The rumor is that Nachman is so angry she's planning to install video cameras to keep an eye on the students."

"No way!" I exclaimed. I was stunned by how far this had gone. "She's going to spy on us? That's terrible."

"Indeed. My thoughts exactly."

"First metal detectors, now this. She's turning this school into some kind of prison or something. What's next? Fingerprinting?"

"Precisely."

"Cameras!" I sputtered. "What about our rights? Our privacy? What about—" I stopped mid-rant. Stopped talking and walking.

Melody turned when she noticed I was no longer beside her. "Casey?"

Ms. Nachman wasn't the only one who wanted to catch the election saboteur. And she had just given me the perfect way to do it—just in time for the *Real News* deadline!

Tape Wins Goofiest School-Video Contest!

WEDNESDAY. AFTER SCHOOL, I met up with Ringo and Melody. I had made a quick run home to pick up the video camera. I told Gram I was using it for a school project. I just failed to mention that the project was self-assigned and that I planned to the leave the brand-new camera in school overnight.

Ringo was so used to all his cheerleader tricks that he had no problem boosting up Melody and helping her stay balanced. Once she was in place, I handed her the camera. I had already set the timer. The camera would shut off when school closed, then it would restart early tomorrow, just before school started again.

We positioned the camera above the lockers in the main hall. Melody aimed it right at the wall where the new posters hung. The way I figured it, if the culprit struck again, it would be here. They were going for maximum effect with minimal effort.

"You can let me down now," Melody said.

"Righto," Ringo said. Melody grabbed my hands and steadied herself. She came back down to earth.

"The top of those lockers is really filthy," she complained.

She was right. She had left grime all over my fingers. I wiped my hands on my jeans. Melody wiped hers on Ringo.

"Now what, Secret Agent Casey?" Ringo said.

"This *is* kind of like *Mission Impossible*," I said. "Step one has been completed. Surveillance in place." Now I just hoped something would show up on the videotape.

"If you don't catch the bad guys, maybe you'll have something for that show *Goofiest Home Videos*," Ringo said.

"If I don't catch the bad guys, the election may be canceled and I'll have no front-page story," I said.

Okay, so I'm not sure which mattered to me more. They were both biggies in my book.

Thursday morning, I yanked on my jeans, sweater and blue Converse hightops and raced to school. Ringo was waiting for me. We were so early, the security guard hadn't arrived yet. The metal detector wasn't even turned on. Luckily they were still only in the "experimental phase."

"They struck again!" Ringo cried. "Willa Greenberg's big poster is gone!"

"And we caught the culprit on videotape!" I high-fived Ringo.

This was so cool! We had just solved the mystery, had the evidence and had time to spare to get it all into the paper.

We raced over to the lockers. Ringo quickly boosted me up to reach the camera. Luckily it was still there. I don't know what I would have done if it had disappeared.

We rushed to the media center and I signed up for a VCR. I couldn't wait to watch my personal version of *Candid Camera*. I popped in the tape and pressed play.

"There's us!" Ringo said. "You don't think *we* had anything to do with this, do you?"

The video showed Ringo, Melody and me horsing around after we planted the camera. That was yesterday afternoon. After a while, the screen blinked, and we saw the empty hall at early morning.

I sat at the edge of my seat waiting to catch the culprits.

Oh no. My eyes widened. Willa Greenberg's poster just fell down. All by itself. The edge curled up, and the poster dropped onto the floor. Nothing incriminating other than a piece of dried-up masking tape. There went my big scoop.

I hit the Stop button and sighed. "Well, that was a total waste."

"Not total," Ringo said. "It gave me an idea." He held up a sketch pad.

WE'RE WATCHING YOU!

"Excellent," I said. "Too bad I can't come up with something equally good."

The rest of the morning's classes were canceled so we could all attend the election assembly. With all the weirdness surrounding the campaigns, the assembly might actually be interesting. School safety and the metal detectors had to be one of the main topics.

Since I had the camera with me, I figured I might try my hand at filming a documentary again. I hoped sitting down would make handling the camera easier.

I found a seat near the front. A bunch of the yearbook crowd sat in front of me. Not one even bothered to say hi or glance in my direction. I guess I was too insignificant.

Spencer Woodham was up onstage. Since he was the current president, he introduced each of the candidates. Willa got a lot of applause. Jodi barely registered. That made me feel bad. I clapped really hard for her so that it would sound louder. Dave got cheers from his Brain-Busters buddies. Natalie got whoops from the jock circle.

Here's a question: How come when jocks cheer for someone they always make animal noises?

"First, we'll have the presidential candidates explain why they think they would be the best person for the job," Spencer announced. "Then I will ask a question they each will have a chance to answer. After that, all the other candidates will introduce themselves."

I balanced the camera to scribble down some notes. It was awkward.

"This is ridiculous," I muttered. I gave up on using the camera. I popped on the lens cap and lay the camera on the seat beside me.

Willa was up first. She gave Spencer a huge smile and then faced the auditorium. She was totally confident.

"Hello, fellow students, teachers and administrators," she said, beaming. The girl practically glowed.

"I will make the best student council president for so many reasons. I have been super-involved in everything that goes on here ever since the sixth grade. If I were president I'd schedule more school dances. Extra-special menu days. Believe me, a vote for me is really a vote for yourselves."

She was so smooth you'd think she'd actually said something.

I felt really bad that Jodi had to follow her. Jodi would have had a tough time anyway, because she's really shy, but following Willa might make her look worse. The yearbook clique in front of me whispered and giggled as she stepped up to the podium.

I accidentally on purpose kicked the back of the chair in front of me. Hard.

One of the yearbookies turned around and glared at me.

I made a face. "Sorry," I whispered.

"Um, hi," Jodi mumbled into the mike. "I would like to be your student council president because I really care about all the issues." She took a deep breath and clutched the podium. Her voice was much stronger when she began again. "Sometimes it's hard for kids to be heard—especially if they're like me. Shy. Not one of the popular crowd. Well, if I was the student council president, I'd make sure everyone had a chance to make their views known. You have a voice, and I'm here to make sure you're heard."

Off to my right, a group of guys stopped mumbling and faced the stage. Even the year-bookies in front of me were listening. Shy, beige Jodi had gotten their attention.

"We all have different opinions, but we can meet in the middle," Jodi went on. "If we work together, we can make Trumbull a good place to be. A school for every student. A school for you."

Way to go, Jodi. I clapped really hard as she returned to her seat.

Dave Tyson kind of glared at Jodi. I guess he was bugged that she made such a good pitch. He strode to the podium. "I'm Dave Tyson. I'm smart and I play to win. And if you vote for me for president I'll be sure to win for all of you."

Dave had a definite spark. But as he kept

talking I kept thinking how canned he sounded. Rehearsed. Still, I thought, glancing around, he had a lot of kids applauding.

Natalie bounced over to the microphone. "Hi, everybody," she said.

"Hi, Natalie," one of the jocks called back.

"I'm not going to make a speech," she said.

Was this going to be one of those "I'm not here to make a speech" speeches?

"I'm just announcing that I'm dropping out of the election," Natalie said. "So whatever you do, don't vote for me!"

There was a stunned gasp. Talk about a scoop! Too bad everyone already knew it.

"I realized that being president is a lot of responsibility," Natalie explained. "So is being on the swim team. We have a shot at making the junior championship this year. I don't want to let my teammates down. Being president would really cut into my training time. But thanks, everybody."

She waved at the crowd and sat back down.

Interesting. It was now a three-way race. And from the looks of things, it was now a lot closer than anyone—especially Willa—ever imagined it would be.

Spencer Woodham walked back over to the podium. "Well, that was a shocker," he said to the audience. "Settle down, everyone, we still have our question for the candidates."

I wondered what he was going to ask. I hoped it wasn't the usual fluff—like if you were an animal what animal would you be.

I was amazed. He actually asked the candidates their position on the proposed metal detectors.

Willa was up first again. She smoothed her hair, then leaned toward the mike. "Well, Spence," she said, as if he was the only person who mattered in the room. "I think we need to be protected from anyone who might hurt us. The administrators know what they're doing—they're grown-ups. We should do all we can to cooperate. What's a little inconvenience in light of the tragedies in other schools?"

I checked out the reactions of the crowd. From what I could tell, the only kids who were clapping were the Willa wannabees.

Jodi seemed a little more comfortable this time. "We need to find the right balance between safety and freedom. That means we must take the time to examine the issue from all sides. I do feel the students should have a chance to air their views. After all, we're the ones who will be most affected by these decisions."

Sensible. Maybe she really did have a chance.

Then Dave got up and gave a fiery speech. He sure knew how to whip up the crowd.

"This is our school!" he boomed. "It's up to us how to run things. We can't let them push us around, invading our turf. We may be kids, but we have rights!"

He got a lot of cheers. Willa looked pale. And really, really annoyed. Her applause meter registered that she wasn't doing all that well against her opponents.

Next the student reps started talking, and that's when I zoned out. The girls in front of me whispered and dissed any of the candidates who weren't their friends. Predictable.

I scoped out the auditorium. I spotted Johnny Ryan leaning against the back wall. He looked totally bored. Also predictable.

Megan scurried from one seat to another. Probably trying to get a better view of Spencer.

"What a drip," a yearbook girl said in front of me.

I wondered who she was talking about.

"She's such a Goody Two-Shoes," the other girl agreed. "I don't get why Spence likes her."

Whoa! I sat up straight. Were these girls talking about Megan? Or did Spence like some other girl? Either way, the yearbook clique had my full attention.

"Willa's plan is really working," the first girl said. "Inviting Megan along has made Spence hang around more."

"When is Willa going to swoop in and steal him away from that teacher's pet?" the other girl wondered. "I'm so over hanging around with the babies."

"She's going to wait until Spence is around. Then she's going to make a total fool out of that girl. Right in front of Spence. There's no way he'll keep liking Megan after Willa gets done with her." The girl laughed, really meanly. "Willa has already been dropping hints to him that Megan isn't the sweet, smart girl he thinks she is."

"Willa is so awesome," the second girl said. Then she shuddered. "I don't ever want to cross her."

I couldn't believe it. Megan sincerely believed those girls were her friends, and all they wanted to do was humiliate her. And why? Over some boy. Megan was going to be incredibly hurt when she found out they were just using her to get to Spence. I knew those dimwits were mean, but this was too vicious.

I opened my mouth to slam the girls when I realized they didn't know Megan was a friend of

mine. I mean, that I knew her. Whatever. I didn't
want to clue them in that I was onto Willa's totally
harsh plan. I wanted to warn Megan.

The only problem was: Would Megan believe me?

CHAPTER 19

Surveys Show: No One Listens to Bad News!

MEGAN ALWAYS TRIES to believe the best about everyone. It was totally possible that she would accuse me of making up this stuff because she knew I didn't like Willa and that crowd. I wasn't even sure of the names of these girls I had overheard.

The speeches over, the girls in front of me hurried down to congratulate Willa, Stacy and Katherine.

I packed up and realized—the video camera! The little red Record light was still on. I had forgotten to turn it off! I had put on the lens cap, so there wouldn't be any picture. But there would be very revealing audio.

I had to get this tape to Megan. It was the proof I needed.

I bit my lip. People had a habit of blaming the messenger. Should I leave her the tape anonymously? Maybe slip it into her "JAM" box so she didn't wail on me for bringing the bad news?

Get real, I told myself. There was no way she'd think it was anyone but me. How many other kids just happened to bring a video camera to school lately?

I spotted Megan down in front surrounded by Willa and the other two-faced traitors. Megan fiddled with her hair and smiled up at Spence. Now was not the time.

But when?

At lunch the buzz was all about Natalie dropping out and how well Dave and Jodi did. Some of the other class reps had made an impact too— and not just the popular kids. It looked like this might be the year of the underdog candidate.

I didn't see Megan anywhere.

As I passed by Willa and Stacy's table I suddenly heard a lot of whispering. Then giggling. I glanced over. They were definitely talking about me.

I marched right over. "Do you have something you want to say to me?" I demanded.

Willa never lost her cool. "Never. Why would I want to waste my time talking to you?" She purposefully turned her back on me and started talking to Stacy. As if I wasn't even standing there.

She really thinks she's all that, I thought.

Kids glanced over from other tables. More whispers. More giggles. I felt like a freak.

They were snubbing me. Well, so what? As if that was news. I could snub them, too!

Of course, it was hard to snub someone who wasn't paying attention. I spent lunch alone, acting as if I didn't care.

Which I didn't. Really. In fact, it fueled my flame. I couldn't wait until I exposed that two-faced traitor for what she was. She'd be sorry she messed with me. Or Megan.

I planned to make sure of that.

I didn't see Megan again that afternoon. Every time I popped my head into the *Real News* office I had just missed her. I didn't pass her in the halls. The only thing I could do was stop by her house after school.

I went home to check in with Gram. It's one of those things a kid has to do now and then—even with my flexible Gram. Let her know I'm still alive. Doing homework. Need dinner. That kind of thing. It makes them feel like they're doing their parental duties.

"Ready for the PTA meeting?" Gram asked.

Oh, man! I slapped my head to my forehead. I had forgotten all about it. I needed to get the inside scoop on the metal detectors. But I felt as if I would explode if I didn't talk to Megan.

I hopped from one foot to the other, trying to decide. PTA or Megan? PTA or Megan.

"Do you have to go to the bathroom?" Gram asked.

"No, but I do have to go somewhere," I said. "You have to promise me that you will tell me every single detail so I can write it up."

"What's so urgent that you'll miss investigating a story?" Gram asked, one eyebrow raised.

"It *is* a story," I said. A story about traitors. "I have to go talk to Megan about it."

Gram swore on her journalism awards to fill me in on everything. Then I tossed the videotape into my backpack and booked it over to Megan's.

I rang the bell. Megan answered the door. She looked puzzled.

"Casey? What are you doing here?"

"I need to talk to you about something." I pushed my way past her into the hallway. "It's important."

"I'm on my way out," Megan said. "Can I call you later?"

Willa and Stacy stepped into the hallway. "Got your coat?" Willa asked. "Oh. Hello, Casey."

"We're on our way to the mall," Megan explained. "Willa saw a dress at Buzz that she thinks would look perfect on me."

"It's pale pink," Stacy added. As if it was important.

I ignored her. I concentrated only on Megan. "Megan, I think you really want to hear this. You may want to rethink your plans."

Megan's mom came into the hall. "Are you ready to go?" she asked. "Megan, grab your coat, honey."

"I need to talk to Casey for one minute," Megan said. "I'll be right out."

Victory! But I could tell Willa and Stacy didn't want to leave Megan alone with me.

Megan's mom solved my problem. "Come on, girls," Mrs. O'Connor said to Willa and Stacy. "Let's warm up the car."

I waited until they were safely out the door. "Listen, Megan. Willa and Stacy are seriously bad news."

"I know you don't like them." Megan said. "But they're my friends, and you can't tell me who I can or can't be friends with."

"That's not what I'm —"

Megan cut me off. But she did it in this sickeningly sweet voice. "Casey, I know it's been kind of hard on you that the older girls haven't included you. I'm sorry if that hurt your feelings. I should have been more sensitive. I really didn't mean to neglect our friendship."

My eyes bugged. "Our *what*?"

"I have been kind of caught up in all of this," she had the nerve to continue. "I promise, I will spend more time with you."

"You think . . . You believe . . . I . . ." I was so mad and frustrated that I think I sprayed her with spit while I sputtered partial sentences.

"I really have to go now. My mom only agreed to take us to the mall on a school night because I promised it would be a quick trip."

"Have a wonderful time with your wonderful best friends," I spat. I stormed out.

I couldn't believe it! I gave up the PTA meeting for this? She actually thought I was jealous. That the whole problem was that I wished she was with me instead of with them. Or that I cared that she was their "chosen one."

What planet was she living on? Megan and I weren't really friends. We worked together on a mutual project. Like those birds who hang out with hippos to eat the insects that land on their backs. Symbiotic—if you want to know the advanced vocabulary word for it. Yin and yang. Wait, now I'm moving into Ringo territory.

But by the time I got home, I wasn't fuming over Megan's misunderstanding anymore. I was feeling sorry for her. She really believed that those two girls liked her. She thought they were friends—*real* friends. Like, tell-all-your-secrets-and-spill-your-guts gushy girlfriends. And those girls were going to spill Megan's guts all over the floor. They were going to use anything they could to embarrass her, and Megan was clueless.

It wasn't going to be a pretty sight. And no matter how much she irked me, I had to do anything I could to prevent it.

The problem was, the only way Megan was going to believe me was by hearing that tape. I'd have to wait until tomorrow.

I hoped it wouldn't be too late.

CHAPTER 20

Studies Prove Too Much Hairspray Affects Brain Cells!

LATER THAT NIGHT, I was doing math homework at the kitchen table when Gram came in from the PTA meeting. Her hair was pulled back with a black comb, and her eyes were shining with news.

"The metal detectors were voted down by a huge majority," Gram announced. "But not without some heated discussion."

"I need details!" I crowed. "I've got to turn in my story tomorrow. Did parents argue? Did Ms. Caldwell pitch a hissy fit? Was there mud wrestling? Or a food fight?"

"Amy Caldwell tried to present the whole issue of metal detectors as if it was her gift to the school. She'd spent so many hours researching companies, and so many hours at school checking with the security guard. Ha! Her gift turned

179

out to be a major goose egg."

"Did you make a speech?" I asked, wishing I had been there.

"I said my share. But Amy and the advocates of heightened security were clearly outnumbered, thank goodness. I don't think I could have restrained myself if there had been a hundred Amy Caldwells in the auditorium."

"I'm sorry I missed it," I said. Especially since my visit to Megan's house had been a bust. Still, I'd tried. "Maybe I can get a copy of the minutes from the PTA meeting. But it won't be in time for tomorrow's deadline."

Gram opened her bag and waved a little portable tape recorder at me. "I got it all on tape for you." She popped out the tape and handed it to me. "My gift to you."

"You're the best gram in the world!" I grabbed the tape and kissed her cheek. "Thanks."

"I'm just relieved that reason prevailed, and the metal detectors are on their way out."

"Not a minute too soon. Everyone was getting jittery from the bells and lights that kept going off—all day and all the time."

Gram dropped one hand onto my shoulder. "Let's just hope metal detectors will remain an unnecessary evil at Trumbull—and at all schools."

I ran upstairs to transcribe the tape and finish

my story on school safety. But even after I'd input my story, finished my homework and jumped in the shower, I had trouble sleeping. I alternated between being mad at Willa and Stacy, and mad at Megan for being so blind. All in all, not a good night.

When I arrived at school Friday morning, election mania was in full swing.

"Dave Tyson! The smart choice!" I heard Dave's voice blaring all around me, but I didn't see him. Then a car rounded the corner. Dave's head poked out of the sunroof. He was shouting campaign slogans through a bullhorn.

Practically every few feet someone shoved a flyer into my hand. A group of girls paraded in front of the school carrying posters saying "Willa Greenberg for President." Jodi stood by the entrance wearing a "Jodi Dillard for President" T-shirt and cap, answering questions. She had printed up flyers with her position on everything from school security to lunch menus.

I took one of Jodi's flyers. "Good luck," I told her.

"Thanks," she said. She glanced around, then leaned in and whispered, "Do you think I have a chance now?"

I smiled. "You've got my vote." I even meant it.

Just as Gram promised, the front entrance was minus one malfunctioning metal detector. I decided to get the voting over with. We could vote during any free period, and then the votes would be tallied after school.

I wasn't the only one who was going to vote before class. The gym was packed.

Here was the system: There was a "No Personal Articles in the Voting Area" rule, so kids dropped off their backpacks and stuff with teachers at a table. Then each kid picked up a ballot and went over to one of the ballot boxes. To teach us about "real" voting, they had set up booths with curtains. We didn't get to pull levers or anything, but it was kind of cool to step inside and drop a ballot into the slot. My very first middle-school election.

I checked off Jodi for president. She had made good points in the assembly, and really thought about the issues. Dave actually kind of scared me—he was so competitive and power crazy. And Willa? Hah!

I checked off candidates for other offices, candidates I believed actually might truly represent all kids, and slipped my ballot into the box.

I pushed open the curtains. "All done," I announced to Mr. Fitchberg. He was the teacher assigned to my booth.

"Thank you for participating in the electoral process," he said. Gee. Even normal conversation sounded like advanced English class with this guy.

There was some kind of commotion a few tables over. A shriek startled me. "She fainted!" someone yelled.

Mr. Fitchburg leapt to his feet. A crowd gathered, making it hard for me to see. I finally understood high heels. They improve visibility.

I squeezed through to the front. Two teachers were helping Katherine Cutter to her feet. Her legs were all wobbly.

"What happened?" I asked the girl standing next to me.

"She fainted. One minute she was vertical, the next, she was horizontal."

"I think it's the stress from the election," a guy behind me said. "It totally wigged her out."

Stacy Carmel pushed through the crowd. She hugged Katherine. "Are you okay?" she squealed.

Katherine nodded and leaned heavily against Stacy.

"Come along, dear," one of the teachers said. "We need to get you to the nurse."

"I'm fine, really," Katherine protested faintly. "I don't know what happened."

"It's that silly diet of yours," Stacy scolded

loudly. "I bet she didn't have any breakfast this morning," Stacy told the teacher. "Do you think that could be why she fainted?"

Angling to get out of morning classes is the more likely reason, I thought.

"Nothing more to see here," Coach Tickner boomed. "Move along. The first bell is about to ring."

The crowd scattered.

I had taken care of voting. Now I needed to take care of things with Megan. But once again, my morning classes got in the way. Unless I got lucky and snagged Megan in the hall, I'd have to wait till lunch.

There's one thing Megan is, and that's predictable. I knew she'd stop by her locker during lunch.

I raced to her locker the minute the bell rang. I paced in front of it, waiting.

"Come on," I muttered. I felt in my backpack for the videotape for the millionth time. I needed to grab Megan, drag her to the library, and make her see what sewer rats those girls really were.

This wasn't going to be fun. I would be glad when it was all over.

Spence Woodham strolled toward me. "Are you waiting for Megan, too?" he asked. "We were going to meet here and then go to lunch."

I stared at him. He and Megan were at the lunch-date stage? Middle-school kids made lunch dates?

"Hi, Spencer," Willa Greenberg cooed. Yes. You read that right—she cooed. My stomach gurgled, and it wasn't because it was lunchtime.

"Hi, Willa," he said.

"I just came to tell you Megan won't be meeting you for lunch after all."

"Oh?"

Willa smiled, each dimple a totally treacherous pothole. "There's some crisis in the yearbook office. Megan's all caught up in it. I guess she just thought that was more important than meeting you." She shrugged and made a face that made it clear how foolish she thought Megan was for passing up the opportunity to fawn over Spencer.

Willa linked her arm through Spencer's and practically dragged him away.

Hm. I wondered if Willa had something to do with that crisis. Yeah. Just like I wondered if Buffy was going to slay some vampires every week. No-brainer.

Willa is going to be sorry she messed with a friend of mine, I fumed.

Friend? I caught myself.

Whatever.

Final Election Outcome
Isn't So Final!

I HAD A new plan. I was covering the election, so I had to be in the gym after school when the votes were tallied. I had a sneaking suspicion Megan would be there, too. School events like this were kind of a magnet for her. She couldn't stay away.

Besides, I had a feeling Spencer would be there. I remembered something about the out-going president monitoring the votes for the in-coming. That would clinch Megan's presence. The only problem was, Willa might be there too. I had to get Megan alone.

Megan nodded coldly at me when I entered the gym. Could Willa have said something to her? Some lie to make it seem as if I was the bad guy here?

All too possible.

I plopped down beside her. "Hey," I said.

"Hi." She did not greet me with a patented perky hello. There was a definite chill in the air. Siberian freeze. I had to proceed with caution, like a driver on an icy road. One wrong turn, and wipeout.

Anything I said now she'd chalk up to jealousy or a vendetta. I had to somehow get her to hear the tape, or I didn't have a shot.

"Megan," I began. Then I stopped, not sure where to go from there.

"Sh," she said. "They're starting to count the ballots. We don't want to distract them."

I pulled out my notebook to keep track of the tally. I wondered where Spencer was. Had Willa kidnapped him to keep him away from Megan?

Finally the teachers began counting the votes for president. They started with votes for Willa. My stomach clenched. I so hoped she hadn't won.

The first teacher counted batches of ballots. Then the ballots were handed over to the next teacher to be recounted. Twenty. Twenty more. Then twenty more. Willa was winning by a land-slide.

I doodled around the numbers I'd written down. How long was this going to take? Then I did a double-take. Something about the numbers looked wrong.

I added up the columns. Willa already had nearly three hundred votes. But there was still another whole box to be counted.

I wrote a note to Megan:

How many kids are enrolled at Trumbull?

Megan read the note and looked perplexed. Then she wrote:

318. I think. It might be 320.

Either way, these numbers were way off. Which could only mean one thing.

I leaped to my feet. "Stop counting!" I shouted.

"Casey!" Megan hissed beside me.

The teachers glanced up. Severe annoyance times three.

"Casey, what is the meaning of this interruption?" Ms. Nachman demanded.

I dashed over to the table. "I'm really sorry, but this is important. This election was rigged!"

I showed her the numbers in my notebook. "See? There are more votes than there are kids. Someone stuffed the ballot boxes!"

Trio Falls from Top of Popularity Pyramid!

MS. NACHMAN LOOKED stunned. Then she looked serious. Her whole face flattened into a straight-lined frown.

"Girls, can you excuse us?" she said. "We need to recount these ballots, and then decide what to do."

"Can I come back and get the story for *Real News*?" I asked.

I knew I was pushing it, but I'm a reporter first, mild-mannered student second. Okay, I'm never a mild-mannered student.

"Casey," Ms. Nachman said in a warning tone. But she didn't say no, so I took it as a yes.

"Wow," Megan said as I followed her into the corridor. "I don't believe it. Someone actually stuffed the ballot box. That's so wrong. I can't

190

believe someone we know would do something like that."

"Uh, sometimes you don't know people as well as you think you do," I said.

"I guess." She gave me a sideways glance. "We've sometimes been wrong about each other."

"Megan, there's something I've been trying to show you. Please, please come with me to the media center."

She looked at me a little suspiciously. Then she shrugged. "Well, we have to wait around for Ms. Nachman to finish anyway."

We went into the media center and signed up for a VCR. I reached into my backpack and grabbed a tape. I shoved it into the machine before Megan could change her mind.

I hit Play, and waited for the thing to cue up. "Willa is so not your friend," I blurted.

Megan covered her ears. "Casey, we've been over this before. I don't want to hear mean things—"

I yanked her hands down. "I'm just trying to tell you the truth. And sometimes the truth hurts. I don't want it to. That's just how it is."

She stared at me, so I let go of her wrists.

She glanced at the video screen. "Why are you playing me a tape of lockers?" Megan asked.

I whipped my head around. "Oh, no! I grabbed

the wrong tape from home." It was the video I had made with Ringo and Melody. The one that proved that some brands of masking tape were better than others.

"This isn't the tape I thought it was, but you have to listen to me," I said. "The tape I wanted to play was a recording I accidentally made about a nasty plan of Willa's. About you."

Megan's eyes widened. I had her hooked now. "About me?"

"Megan, they're just using you," I told her. "They are not nice people. You are so much better than they are."

I was laying it on a little thick. I wanted to soften the blow. That's all.

I explained everything. How they were playing her for a sucker to get to Spence. How Willa planned to make her look like a geekazoid in front of him. That they were only pretending to like her.

Megan never took her eyes off the video screen. I could tell this was supertough for her to hear. Her jaw kept popping as she gritted her teeth.

"Let me ask you something," I said. "Today, you were supposed to meet Spencer for lunch, right?"

She nodded. She couldn't face me.

"But you didn't, right?"

"Willa needed me to fix something in the year-book computer program." Her voice was soft. I could tell the news was all sinking in. That couldn't feel good.

"Well, Willa showed up for that lunch instead of you. She told Spence you had more important things to do."

Megan pressed her lips together. Her blue eyes were a little shinier than normal. Hearing that someone you thought was a friend was actually plotting against you—I couldn't think of anything more barfsome.

"I . . . I didn't do this to upset you," I said. "I had to stop them. I wasn't going to let them do that to you."

Megan's jaw dropped open in shock. I didn't see why. I mean, was it so unbelievable that I would try to stick up for her? Well, yes it was.

Then I realized she was staring at something on the screen. I turned to see it.

The video didn't show an empty hall of lockers anymore. Willa, Stacy and Katherine stood there talking in low voices. The microphone barely picked up what they were saying. Only a few words came through.

"I don't know . . ." Katherine said. She seemed uncomfortable.

"Look," Willa snapped. That was easy to hear.

"Get with the program. You're already in deep."

Willa handed little stacks of papers to Stacy and Katherine.

"What is she giving them?" I asked. "Cue cards for obnoxious things to say? Lists of her favorite hair products?"

"Ballots." Megan declared. "Those look like voting ballots."

She hit the Pause button.

We studied the screen. She was right.

My heart sped up. We had just found evidence that Willa and her pals stuffed the ballot boxes. It all made sense.

"Willa and Stacy are already in student council," Megan reasoned. "It's possible they got their hands on a blank ballot."

"All they had to do was make multiple copies. But how?"

"The yearbook committee has a copier," Megan said. "Willa and Stacy could have found a time when no one was around. No one would think twice if they were in there."

"You know what?" I said. "I bet they were the ones sabotaging the election all along. They probably posted those notes about Katherine to throw us off their trail. And it almost worked."

"But how did they get all the extra ballots into the boxes?" Megan wondered. "They'd never sneak them past the teachers."

I thought about that, then snapped my fingers as it hit me. "I know how. By creating a diversion." I filled Megan in on Katherine's fainting fit. "No one would have noticed if Willa and Stacy snuck into the booth together. Or went in with stacks of ballots tucked into their clothes." I wasn't exactly sure which one of those things they did, but I knew it was definitely one of them. Katherine's faint had looked fake to me all along.

"Can we prove this?" I wondered.

"I think we can," Megan said, her blue eyes flashing with resolve. She pulled a folder out from her books. It was labeled *Yearbook* in glitter letters. She flipped it open. "The yearbook copier makes those funny lines, remember? It's why we were going to buy a new one."

"Wait a sec!" I just remembered. I had saved the "Jodi Dull-ard" note that Jodi had handed me in the bathroom. I had scribbled some story ideas on the back of it. I pulled it out and turned it over.

"Ta-dah!" The incriminating shadowy line. Right there in gray and white.

"We have to tell Ms. Nachman."

We raced back to the gym. Ms. Nachman and the other teachers were packing up.

"You were right, Casey." Ms. Nachman told me. "There are far more ballots than students."

She looked really sad. She shook her head. "I don't know why this election got so out of hand."

I wished I could answer that question myself. "We know who did it," I announced. "Maybe *they* can tell you."

Megan and I showed Ms. Nachman our evidence. The tape. The note with the line down the back. Now for the clincher.

Ms. Nachman flipped the ballots over. Dozens of them had the line running down the back. All of those had Willa Greenberg, Stacy Carmel and Katherine Cutter checked off as the candidates of choice.

"Do you know where these girls are now?" Ms. Nachman asked Megan.

Megan nodded. "They were planning a victory party in the yearbook meeting room."

Unbelievable. "Of course they already planned it," I said. "Because they knew they would win by cheating."

Ms. Nachman sent her assistant to fetch the girls. I was really glad that she didn't ask us to leave.

I hoped Megan would hold up under the pressure. I had to admire her—she was a tougher cookie than her vanilla-frosting exterior made her look.

Willa, Stacy and Katherine came into the gym.

They seemed nervous.

They confessed all. Of course they did. We had the evidence to back up the accusations.

"It's not fair," Stacy whined. "It's our last year. We deserve to be on student council."

"We were sure we would win," Willa said. "Who would oppose us? Then all these other kids got into the act."

I was stunned. I think Ms. Nachman was pretty stunned, too.

I have to admit, I felt a little smug. Willa and Stacy had never been hauled down to the guidance counselor's office during all of this. Why? Because Ms. Nachman had bought into the whole popularity game. Now maybe she would see the error of her ways, and cut me, Ringo and other nonconformists some slack.

Katherine looked miserable. "Don't you see? If we're not popular, what are we?"

"Precriminals," I muttered.

Megan elbowed me. She wasn't the type to revel in someone else's misfortune, despite the fact that these girls had tried to ruin her life. Sometimes Megan was so perfect it scared me.

But Katherine's sad lament reminded me of the conversation I'd had with Griffin. I actually felt sorry for this rotten trio. Not because they lost the election or their footing at the top of the popularity food chain, but because they thought that this dinky little election was all that they had.

The one I felt sorriest for was Katherine. I'd seen the way Willa and Stacy bossed her around. She'd taken it, just so she could remain in their orbit. Look where it had gotten her.

"Stop the presses!" I shouted as I ran into the newsroom.

Okay. So there aren't really any presses in the news office. But I had seen that in a movie once and had been waiting for the perfect moment to say it. This was it.

Toni and Ringo were there, waiting to slide the election results into our next issue of *Real News*. Ringo looked up from the computer. "You have the election results?"

"I have a new front-page election story!" I cheered. Over at Dalmatian Station, Toni groaned.

Megan came in behind me. "Stop enjoying this so much, Casey," she said.

I wanted to hold back. I really did. I knew this whole thing was bumming Megan out. But this was some story. Maybe even worthy of an expanded version of *Real News* instead of a shrunken one.

"Front page?" Toni repeated. "We already laid

out the whole issue. Are you for real?"

I glanced at Megan.

"She's for real," Megan said. "This is definitely a front-page story. Which means we have a lot of work to do."

I sat at the computer, and my fingers flew across the keys. I barely heard the grumbles around me.

"I'll fill you in on the details as I get them," Megan said. She dashed back down the hall to Ms. Nachman's office.

I looked around the newsroom. Everyone was engrossed, working together. I took in a deep, satisfying breath. I did have a place where I belonged. It was right here.

Megan dashed back into the office. "Okay," she said, talking fast. "Here's the deal. Stacy, Katherine and Willa are suspended. When they come back, they're off all committees. The election will be rerun on Monday without them."

"Got it," I typed the info into the story.

"Hey, Casey," Ringo said, waving his notebook. "I forgot to tell you, I got some quotes for your story. I went around and asked different kids who they thought was popular."

"You did a poll?" I asked.

"Nah, I just asked questions. But the funny thing was, most of the kids thought the group they hung with was the best group."

"Really?" Toni's eyebrows rose.

"Yeah, like Anna Zafrani and the drama club? They thought the school election was for boring people. And the kids into the election thought the drama club kids were kind of extreme."

Ringo lay down on Dalmatian Station and gazed up at the ceiling.

"I guess the people I need to be popular with are my buds. And I'm happy to say I am an equal-opportunity hanger-outer."

I smiled at him. "I'm glad you are, too!"

Trumbull Students Vote—
One More Time!

Dateline: Monday evening . . . Yeah, I
know. It's a school night, and I'm actually
voluntarily heading over to school for
a—gasp—basketball game.
No, I haven't had a brain overhaul.
Gram and I packed up the video cam
with the tape for Mom and went to the
post office to send it off. The post
office is near school, and anyway, Ringo
is cheering again. He's all excited
because he and Angelina worked up a

special cheer that would let her
participate even with her sprained
ankle. How could I miss that?
Tyler also happened to drop that he
had volunteered to videotape the game
for the coach. Oh, did I forget to
mention that? No biggie.

I closed up my journal as Gram stopped the
Jeep by the school entrance. Waving good-bye, I
jumped out and headed in. I passed by the Brain-
Busters practice on the way to the gym. My eyes
bugged.

Jodi Dillard stood beside the desk, handing
index cards to Mr. Fitchberg. She must have
become his assistant.

I hoped she'd be able to fit it in now that she
was student council president.

That's right—Jodi had won the runoff election that morning! I was really happy for her. And
for us, too. I really thought she'd make a good
president.

I stepped into the gym and spotted Tyler right
away. He didn't see me. He was all focused on the
equipment. My toes curled up all squishy inside

my purple Converses. He looked pretty cute, all serious and intent with the camera.

I stumbled my squishy toes over to the bleachers. Here I am again, I realized. At a game with no one to sit with.

I glanced around. This time Melody was down in front, doing some weird modern dance moves on the sidelines. The cheerleaders had their own cheerleader. Well, Ringo had his own cheerleader.

I saw Megan, and hesitated. Should I join her? Could I stand that much sweetness? I'd just had a bowl of ChocoBlasts after school—I could go into sugar shock.

Except Megan didn't have her usual pink aura surrounding her. She'd been abandoned by the yearbook clique.

I went over and sat beside her. "Hi. Is this seat saved?"

"Nah." Megan studied her pastel shoelaces. "Casey, I owe you an apology."

My eyebrows raised. Miss Perfection was admitting to being less than perfect?

"You were right all along about Willa and Stacy. I just didn't want to hear it."

"You like to believe the best about everyone," I offered. "Not like me."

"I wish that was the total truth, but it's not." She picked at her silver sparkle nail polish. "I pretended I didn't see or hear some of the catty things Willa did and said. It was like you pegged it. I enjoyed feeling, I don't know, special."

"But Megan, you *are* special," I insisted. Gag. Was that me talking? "You don't need those girls to prove that. You prove it every day." Now where did *that* come from?

Megan's face flushed. "You really think that?"

I nodded. I didn't want to say anything else because I was afraid it would make Megan hug me.

"Ringo really had it right," Megan said. "The only kids you need to be popular with are your friends. Being popular just for the sake of being popular, well, it's not much of a goal."

"And we all know how goal-oriented you are."

Megan laughed. "Oh, and you're not?"

Spence sat down. "Is this seat taken?"

"It is now," I said.

Spence studied me as if he couldn't tell if I was inviting him to join us or telling him to buzz off.

"Did you hear about the election?" Megan asked Spencer.

"Yeah. I'm sure Jodi will make a good president," he said. "I feel bad about Willa, though. I never thought she'd do anything like this."

"Me neither," Megan agreed.

"Well, I had her pegged from the beginning," I said.

Megan and Spence both rolled their eyes.

"Well, I did!" I insisted.

"Anyway, I'm really glad the PTA voted down the metal detectors," Megan said. "And your story about school safety really hit the mark, Casey. Another real eye-opener for a lot of kids."

Spencer nodded. "You never think about something like that—until you have to go through a metal detector every day." He folded his arms and stared out over the noisy, hot gym. "Maybe now that the election is over, school will get back to normal," he said. "Good old quiet Trumbull."

Megan and I looked at each other. Then in unison we chimed:

"GET REAL!"

My Word

by Linda Ellerbee

MY NAME IS LINDA ELLERBEE. As you know by now, part of the story in this book is the result of real events, terrible events in which one or more young people took guns to school and killed people. After these tragic occurrences, what everyone seemed to want to know was how such things could happen and—because we are human—just who was to blame?

Some said it was the fault of the schools. There wasn't enough security. A kid shouldn't be able to bring a gun to school. There should be metal detectors, cops, video cameras in school halls, cafeterias and, sometimes, classrooms. Whatever it takes.

When these measures really began to be taken at many schools, kids had different reactions. Many told me they felt their schools were being turned into jails, but not all felt that was a bad thing. One kid said that if jail was where it was safe to go to school, then that's where she wanted to be. But another kid said he never felt afraid going to school before, but now, when he walked to school and had to pass the police car parked outside, it scared him because it reminded him he "might" be in danger.

Some said the cause of these school shootings was poor parenting. What kind of parent doesn't see signs that their kid is slipping into a desperate state of mind? Why didn't parents raise their kids better? Why didn't they teach them to value human life? Why did they keep guns where kids could get at them? Some simply said it happened because we have too many guns, too many people who have access to guns, and we need laws that control the ownership and use of guns. There was a lot of disagreement over the gun thing. And the parenting thing.

Some said it was all the fault of the media. Too much violence. Too little value. Kids watched too much TV and were online too often, and the media was to blame for sending a message that violence was a way to solve your problems.

Of course the media looked for another answer, one that didn't quite point the finger at the media. And so the following reasoning was born: "kids who killed" were "outsiders who didn't fit in." Therefore, being an outsider was why they killed. "Feeling or being different" made them do it. I saw this on TV, heard it on the radio, read it in the papers and online—and heard it from friends of mine who work in news.

But here's the real deal. I've listened to a whole lot of kids and grownups on this subject and asked them the same question: Do you or did you ever feel like an outsider? And I've yet to find anyone who says they didn't.

See, we all feel like outsiders—some of the time, most of the time or maybe even all of the time. Even the most popular kids you know get these feelings. Trust me on this one. The feeling of being an outsider is so common we can probably call it "normal." Especially at your age. And yet—this is important to remember—99.99% do not take out a gun and shoot people.

However, after the real shootings at real schools in which real people died and real lives were lost, kids who didn't look or dress or sound like everybody else began to be watched—by teachers, counselors, parents and even classmates. There was often an air of suspicion. It is understandable, but it does tend to smother individuality, diversity and the right to go your own way, think your own thoughts . . . I mean as long as you don't hurt others.

So in this book I wanted to take on these issues, even if there is more than one answer to a question and none of the answers is easy. As for the outsider thing, I've felt like an outsider most of my life and I've yet to kill anybody. Which is not to say being an outsider doesn't hurt. It surely does. Been there. Done that. Popularity, however, like fame, is often just a paint job. So what counts is not how popular you are or how many friends you have, but finding a couple of people you like, people you understand who also understand you, and learning to be a friend. And trying to like yourself.

Ringo gets it. He always gets it. He's not into cliques. He's not into cataloging people. He's real. Maybe it would be better if we could all be like Ringo, if we could "get it" and . . . get real.

Girl Reporter Gets the Skinny!

ANGELINA CLUTCHED MY arm. "Wh-what do you think is in there?"

I took a deep breath. I mustered up all the guts I had—which were in shorter supply than I'd expected.

It's not like I thought there was a severed head in there. Not really. But whatever was dripping onto the floor was seriously gross.

I approached the locker. "What's the combination?" I asked.

"Two turns to the left, twenty-three . . ." Angelina began.

I reached for the dial. To my surprise, as soon as I tugged on it, the lock opened.

I glanced at Angelina.

"I swear I locked it," she said.

I took another one of those deep breaths that are supposed to be so calming.

Note to self: Breathing thing a myth!

I swung open the locker. Angelina let out a squeak.

A Barbie in a cheerleader's outfit hung from a hook inside. It looked like it was covered in blood.

I have to admit it. The chocolate cake from lunch did a serious herkie in my stomach.

See? I was paying attention during Ringo's practice.

Angelina sank down onto the floor. She leaned against the row of lockers and covered her face with her hands.

"Creepy," I murmured.